THE FOURTH WIDOW

The Best Defense

Boswell blew out the match he'd used to light the kerosene stove and sat down slowly on a folding chair.

"I been thinking," he told me.

"I could tell."

"It seems to me like you're gonna have to figure out who killed little Flory."

"Yeah? Why me?"

"Well, Orrie Buford's a fine fella in his way, but he ain't smart enough to figure out a mystery and if the real killer ain't found, you're gonna get elected for the part since you're the only ex-con in town."

I had to admit he was probably right.

THE FOURTH WIDOW

HAROLD ADAMS
A CARL WILCOX MYSTERY

THE MYSTERIOUS PRESS

New York • London

MYSTERIOUS PRESS EDITION

Copyright © 1986 by Harold Adams
All rights reserved.

Cover illustration by John Jinks

Mysterious Press books are published in association with
Warner Books, Inc.
666 Fifth Avenue
New York, N.Y. 10103

A Warner Communications Company

Printed in the United States of America

Originally published in hardcover by The Mysterious Press.
First Mysterious Press Paperback Printing: June, 1987

10 9 8 7 6 5 4 3 2 1

To Dick: brother, tutor, and friend.

CHAPTER
1

The knocking was hostile as a kick in the balls and loud as the last call of God. I shoved the pillow off my head, rolled from belly to side and opened my eyes. The green window shade, full of cracks and pinholes, leaked needles of light that ricocheted from the white bureau and wooden floor and lanced straight into my aching skull.

"Wilcox! Open up—this here's the law!"

"Quit kicking the Goddamned door and come on in." My voice sounded like a crow with a cold. My mouth was dry and tasty as a hen-coop floor.

Orrie Buford, Corden's substitute cop, shoved the door open, peered around like a hungry toad and pushed in. If his bay window had been any bigger he couldn't have made it because room two in the Wilcox Hotel barely holds a single bed, a little bureau, one straight-backed chair and midget bedbugs. He glared at the whole layout and it was plain to see every inch of the place outraged him. He glared at me.

"What time'd you get to bed?"

"Just before I fell asleep."

"Don't get smart-assed with me," he yelled, "what time?"

"About one, I'd guess—why?"

"Where'd you go when you left the pool hall?"

"Right here."

"You didn't stop for a leak?"

"Well, sure—"

"Out back?"

"Hell no—the toilet's up here."

"You tellin' me you wasn't out back of the hotel?"

"Why in hell'd I go out there when the can's up here?"

"Somebody seen you out back of the hotel."

"Somebody's a liar—what happened out there?"

"I'll ask the Goddamned questions, Wilcox—you just answer and don't give me no horseshit either."

He was sweating with excitement and even in the darkened room I could see his face was red. He kept his thumbs hooked in his belt, as if he didn't trust his hands loose, and his gun butt jutted from the stiff holster on his fat thigh.

I punched up my pillow and propped my head against it.

"I wasn't out back."

"I think you was. I think you met Flory out there."

"Why'd you figure that?"

"Get into your duds—I'll show you what the booze made you forget, maybe."

It galled me to dress in front of him but between my hangover and worry about Flory, I was too bothered to stand on principle so I pulled on my pants, shirt and shoes and went down the hall with Orrie about three steps behind. Down in the lobby my old man, Elihu, was sitting in his swivel chair by the lobby's front door, smoking a La Fendrich and staring out the east window at First and Main. Ma sat in her rocker by the west wall, facing him, hard at work on the patchwork quilt she was making for her grandson, Hank. Neither of them looked too gay.

As we paraded through, Elihu turned his chair, glared at Orrie and snorted.

"You're making a damned fool of yourself," he said. "Joey'd know better."

2

Joey, the town cop for the past dozen years or more, was in Aquatown's hospital where he'd had his appendix removed.

"I'm sorry, Elihu, but I got to do this my way."

Orrie was great at switching from bully cop to ass-kissing politician. To my old man he was all injured innocence and good intentions.

"No Wilcox ever hit a woman," Ma told him without raising her head.

Despite the defense, I didn't like the way neither of them looked at me but couldn't exactly get sore since they had some reason to figure what I did wasn't always predictable.

I suggested we go through the hotel to the back yard but no, Orrie paraded me out the front door, south on First and west through the break in the privet hedge, along the driveway past the wash shed, the garage and rain barrel and under the clotheslines. Just beyond, under a box elder, an army blanket covered a body. Torkelson, Orrie's occasional deputy, leaned against the tree trunk talking to a cluster of citizens. Everybody turned and eyed me.

A black box elder bug with red trim wandered along the blanket where it bulged of the hip. A few ants scrambled in and out under the blanket edge.

I glanced at Orrie who was watching me, squint-eyed, and then took in the crowd again. Some looked curious, a few were hostile, but mostly they seemed numb.

Before Orrie could decide on his next move, Doc Feeney came bustling up. Doc had a mustache and a little beard so clipped, brushed and shiny it looked painted on. His cheeks were round and dark bags hung under his sharp blue eyes. His forehead bulged over dark brows and his hairline started somewhere near the north pole of his round noggin. A navy blue and white seersucker suit crinkled all over him.

His eyes met mine. "What's this?" he asked.

3

"I don't know."

He said, "Good," nodded at Orrie, went down on one knee and flipped the blanket. I'm not squeamish but one glimpse of the mess that had been Flory's fine head was more than I cared for and I looked back at Orrie. Doc sighed, stood up, took off his coat, handed it to me, rolled up his cuffs and crouched down again. After a few seconds he flipped the blanket over the bloody head and stood up with a grunt.

"There's a handerkerchief in the inside pocket there," he told me. I handed it over and he carefully wiped his hands.

"Bring her up to my office," he told Orrie. "I'll perform an autopsy. Offhand I'd say she was killed by repeated blows to the head with a round weapon—something like your billy club."

Orrie looked down at the club as though expecting to find it gone, then squinted at Doc.

"Was she hit from the front?"

Doc spread his hands. "Front, side and back. She was probably knocked down, then beaten on the ground."

"Well, where was she hit first?"

"On the head."

"You're a big help, Doc."

Doc said he was glad to hear that, put his coat on and walked off. Orrie sent Deputy Torkelson to the courthouse for a stretcher and told the growing crowd to get the hell home. Most of the grown-ups strayed off but a few kids hung around at a distance, whispering. When one giggled all the rest looked shocked.

"You through with me?" I asked Orrie.

He roused himself from a deep gloom and waved his pudgy hand.

"No I ain't. You can give Torky a hand getting Flory over to the Doc's office."

4

"Why me?"

He gave me a long look. " 'Cause you're healthy and you're here."

"You don't look crippled to me—"

"Wilcox, you're in enough trouble already—now you gonna help or not?"

Of course I did. It didn't seem possible a girl as small as Flory could be a burden to two men but by the time we'd hiked the block to Doc's we were both sweating. I took the lower end for the climb upstairs, figuring Torkelson would drop her if it was up to him, and while I rested the stretcher handles on my shoulders I was still low and got most of the weight.

"Maybe you'd ought to test me for a hernia," I told Doc when we'd set the body on his examining table.

"Okay, drop your pants."

"Never mind—you're too damned eager."

"I could bill the village."

"The hell with that—us taxpayers get screwed enough."

"All right—if you can't give me business—give me privacy."

Orrie had ordered me to come back so I went along with Deputy Torkelson who walked a little apart and made a big show of keeping his hand close to his gun butt. I was glad the street was almost deserted.

"Well," said Orrie when I was seated in a straight-backed chair beside his desk, "let's go over a few things. You been out of prison a little over three months—right?"

I nodded.

"How come you came back to Corden?"

"I didn't have enough money to go to Paris."

"Don't wise-ass me, Wilcox—I don't happen to think you're the funniest thing in South Dakota. To me you're just a two-time loser, a boozing bum and a Goddamned disgrace to your folks who're just about the finest people in

5

town. Now, why'd you come back here when you can't get along with your old man, hate the hotel and have busted up with your old gal friend, Jenny?"

It was a hell of an embarrassing question—I'd asked myself the same thing more than once and about all I could come up with was I was getting old and felt the need to coast with people I knew for a while, no matter what a pain in the ass they were to me and me to them.

"Well," I said, "Bertha's food is still the best around and even if I can't stand the old man, he doesn't charge for the room as long as I do chores. Besides, Ma asked me to come back."

"Since when have you done what your ma asked?"

"It's been a while—I figured I was due."

Orrie glared at me for several seconds, then leaned closer.

"Okay—so you come home with your tail between your legs—what the hell—it was cold weather and you were broke. But when summer come, what kept you from hitting the rods again? Your pa hadn't changed, you still had no woman I know of—so what kept you? Wasn't it Flory?"

"Hell no—she was just a kid—damned good-looking and nice to see around but the country's full of girls. Besides, she paid me no more mind than a stray cat—maybe less. As a matter of fact, she didn't seem interested in fellas of any kind. She kept to herself."

"And you didn't try to make out?"

"Sure—I tried kidding her—she just never picked up a thing. You might's well try to tame a robin."

"I seem to recollect that you been getting in trouble because of women all your life," he said, sitting back. "There was that widow-woman who needed money so you hit a jewelry store in the Cities, got caught and did time. And then there was a rancher woman who sweet-talked you into some rustling—"

"Uh-huh. And if you work your recollector hard, you'll notice none of those women were kids—they were widows in need. I always been a man for women in need."

"And you always got in trouble when you were drunk." I shrugged.

"And you was drunk last night."

"You got a great memory."

"Uh-huh." He didn't sound too flattered. "Something I don't remember—how'd you manage to buy that truck you got?"

"I didn't buy it—I won it in a poker game—from Sig Larson."

"Gambling's illegal in South Dakota."

"Okay—I've quit. It's not worth the loss of sleep when somebody pays off with a pile of junk like Sig's truck."

Orrie decided to try a different line.

"Was Flory a good worker?"

"You figure if she wasn't, Ma might've belted her?"

"Funnier things have happened—but no—that ain't what I had in mind. Just answer what I ask, okay?"

"All right—she was okay. She did as she was told and she did it brisk enough to get by."

"But she didn't strain herself any—is that what you're saying?"

"She didn't plan to make a career of slinging hash—hell—she was pretty and she was smart—"

"How'd Bertha get on with her?"

"You get along with Bertha or you don't stay in her kitchen."

"Was they chatty?"

"Naw. Bertha never gets familiar with the help. The hired girl's to boss, not chin with."

"And you never laid her, huh?"

"Who—Bertha? Man, she'd squash me—"

"Flory, damn it."

7

"I wish you wouldn't ask that, it makes me feel awful."

"You mean that I'd think you'd do such a thing?"

"No—that I never had the chance. It was a hell of a waste—"

"Never happened before, huh?"

"What?"

"You didn't get into her pants. You made it with every other girl that worked there."

"That's pretty close—just about every other one. Fifty percent's nothing to brag about but then, some of 'em weren't too choice anyway."

"You'd lay a scarecrow if it had a place you could stick that thing into."

"That's not so—they gotta have life in 'em before I perform."

He snorted, leaned back until his chair was resting against the wall and gave me a mean look.

"How drunk'd you get last night?"

"Just pleasant."

"You could still walk, huh?"

"Probably on water."

"Happy drunk—not mean?"

"I never get mean, just randy and willing, you know that."

"Uh-huh." He was still looking mean. "You know what bothers hell out of me? You never asked who it was that seen you out back last night. How come you don't wonder about that?"

"I figured you was lying. If you weren't, somebody else did. I wasn't out there."

"And you don't care who says otherwise?"

"Orrie, if you're dying to tell me—hop to it."

"I ain't gonna tell you—I ain't gonna have you bullying or threatening my witness."

I'd played enough poker with Orrie to know he pushed a

good bluff but not enough to be sure I'd recognize one, and it worried me that he might really have some arsehole on hand who wanted me stuck with a murder rap.

"If you got a witness, you'd better check him out good," I said. "What the hell was he doing out back?"

"I'm gonna check out everything on this. I'm gonna get the son-of-a-bitch that done this, believe me."

He pushed forward, let the chair forelegs thump on the floor and got up. For a second he stood there, pulling up on the heavy gun belt around his middle while he glared out the front windows overlooking Main. He glared so hard it must have tired him because he came back, sat down and scowled at me.

"Who was you with last night?"

"If you know I was at the pool hall, you know it was with Boswell."

"Just wondered if you could remember. You two are gonna kill yourselfs drinking that rotgut he makes, you know?"

"I doubt it. We been trying for years and haven't managed yet."

"You'll make it all right—if you stay out of jail long enough. Now beat it. And don't leave town—we'll talk again."

I strolled from City Hall to Boswell's shack which sits facing the railroad tracks a couple blocks south of Main. Boswell built the place with railway car lumber and it has a boxcar look except for the front where he put in two sash windows flanking the door. All three openings are a little catty-wampus because he was some snockered when he made the measurements.

Inside was a one-room layout filled with cast-off furniture (some I'd brought from the hotel), cardboard boxes and shelves of preserves he'd put up in the fall. Everything was clutter and confusion except the sink which he kept clear along with a gate-leg table he rarely opened. He told me once if it was open it got covered with stuff and he'd only lose it. Boswell was never fussy about anything else but he didn't like eating with a plate in his lap.

"If you got a jug handy, better stash it," I said. "I been talking with Orrie and he guessed we'd been hitting it last night. It still isn't legal to make you own, you know."

"He can't find nothing here."

I looked around at the clutter and had to agree.

He started to fix a pot of coffee while I sat in the rocker, watching. I knew he wouldn't ask why I'd been talking to Orrie so finally I told him.

Boswell blew out the match he'd used to light the kerosene stove and sat down slowly on a folding chair.

"Flory Fancett?"

"Yeah. Somebody beat her to death. Orrie'd like to pin it on me but he hates to get on the wrong side of Ma."

"Flory," he said, and shook his head. "I remember her comin' to school one January morning with her cheeks all frost bit. Had two little spots there in the center of them red cheeks that was white as snowflakes. She didn't cry. There was water in her eyes but she wouldn't let it go. I touched up the spots with a wet rag dipped in medium cool water. She thought I was just grand clear through spring. A perky little gal, cuter than a bug's rectum, spunkier than a skunk."

Boswell, after retiring from the railroad, had taken the school janitor job and stayed with it six years before they let him go. He spent too much time giving kids comfort to suit the principal.

"All the kids thought you were great all the time," I said. "They didn't know you were just a dirty old man."

"Always loved kids," he said, dreamily. "Never had none of my own."

"If you'd paid less attention to kids and more to women, you could've raised a whole tribe of your own."

"Mebbe," he said, without regret. "Who you figure'd do a girl like Flory in?"

I shrugged and wiped sweat from my forehead. "Why in hell don't you put a window in back of this place so you can get some cross-ventilation?"

It took a moment for him to pull away from Flory's corpse and consider body comforts but after a few seconds he said, "I don't because it's cold more'n it's hot, and cold gets me worse."

The teakettle began to boil and he got up and poured the steaming water into the coffeepot where he'd already measured in fresh grounds and it all stirred and bubbled and made the place smell lovely. When he got it settled with a dollop of cold water he poured and handed me a cup.

"I been thinking," he told me.

"I could tell."

"It seems to me like you're gonna have to figure out who killed little Flory."

"Yeah? Why me?"

"Well, Orrie's a fine fella in his way, but he ain't smart enough to figure out a mystery and if the real killer ain't found, you're gonna get elected for the part since you're the only ex-con in town."

I had to admit he was probably right.

"Besides, Flory wasn't just pretty, she was a real fine girl. Whoever done it to her hadn't ought to get away with it."

"So where do you figure I should start—you know any fellas she was running around with?"

"No, but maybe your nephew, Hank, would."

It did seem likely. Hank spent his summers in Corden, helling around town and now and then helping at the

11

hotel. And God knows, being sixteen and horny as a tom-cat he'd not be likely to overlook anything as choice as Flory just because she was a little older. I decided to have a talk with him.

CHAPTER
2

Ma looked up as I came back into the lobby, and bright-green Gabriel, Pa's favorite canary, cut off in mid-note as if nipped by the sudden frost in the air.

"So," said Ma, without missing a stitch in the quilt across her lap, "you haven't been put in jail this time."

"Cheer up, I might make it yet."

She stopped work and gave me the piercing look that turns Pa's head and squelches the hired help. "I see you can still be flippant even after that poor girl's been murdered under my clothesline and the police suspect my son because of the kind of life he's led—"

"That's what gets you, isn't it? The town talk about your kid—you don't care a rap for that 'poor girl.'"

"I care—but I won't pretend sentiment over a girl I barely knew. I certainly see nothing strange or insensitive about being disappointed that the son I bore has been more a source of grief than pride—"

"Well, pride do go before a fall, I hear—is Hank around?"

Her eyes narrowed. "Why do you want him?"

"I figure maybe he knows what fellas Flory's been running around with lately."

Ma sniffed indignantly and resumed the tiny stitches in the quilt.

"Flory wasn't 'running around' with any fellows. We had a clear understanding on that before I hired her. I let her know she had a reputation as a flirt and that I wouldn't put up with any of that around here. She promised me faithfully that she'd outgrown that—she was determined to make something of herself."

"You telling me she took the nun's veil to work in this dump?"

"Hardly. I didn't ask for that—I'm not simple, you know. She could go out Saturday nights and do as she pleased on Sundays. And she never gave me reason to doubt her—not once—until that night when she didn't get in by twelve. Lord knows she paid heavily for that—"

"You mean the night she was murdered?"

"That's right."

"Well, I bet it taught her a lesson. Where'd you say Hank was?"

"After you were taken over to City Hall, I suggested he go swimming, since it was such a hot day."

"You've always had a fine eye for the weather—but why'd you want him gone just because I was getting grilled at City Hall?"

"I would prefer that he know as little as possible about the sordid side of life."

I looked up at Gabriel in his green cage. He hopped down to his feeder and hit the seeds, ignoring my need for a chorus.

Ma was upset so bad she didn't think to assign me a job before I headed out back where I climbed into the wheezing truck I'd won in a poker game my first month out of stir. After some coaxing I brought it to life and headed south on the graveled road to Antelope.

Once it'd been a fairly respectable lake but the drought had shrunk it to little more than a slough. Townsfolk had dammed up the north end and made a swimming area about half the size of a football field. The south end was shallow for little kids and the rest was deep enough to drown in almost anywhere clear of the steep banks. For a couple weeks the first summer there'd been a concession stand in the parking area but only a handful of kids ever came to swim so it was abandoned and someone towed it off for a hen coop or kindling. The whole project was typical of enterprises tried during the Depression—they all went bust.

Hank's gang was playing water tag along the north bank as I pulled into the parking area. I could hear the yelling even before I turned off my motor. Then they saw me and the moving picture became a snapshot.

Hank's always had mixed feelings about me. Like a lot of smart kids, he's tolerant of his parents but has an exaggerated respect for his grandparents, and the fact that Ma regards me with something less than total admiration makes him uncomfortable about enjoying my kind of humor. Like his grandmother, he believes a man should conduct himself in a way that makes him important to the right people. Hank believes in Family Honor, God and Country. He isn't religious but embraces God because He's on our side. He's a patriot because the country belongs to him and his loyalty goes to anything that's his.

He doesn't approve of me being divorced, a boozer or a jailbird, let alone having a weakness for women and no apparent noble ambitions. I rate a little respect because I paint signs well and can build a bench that won't wobble, but what really impresses him is that I can chin myself with one hand and so far as he knows, I've never lost a fight. Since vanity is another one of my weaknesses, I've never bothered to straighten him out on this last illusion.

As I walked toward them the young people came out of the water and gathered in a group on the high bank, their wet bodies glistening in the sunlight. Then Hank started toward me, like the parley man when Indians and white men meet on the plains.

He had my build from the hips up but his legs were straight so he was nearly two inches taller and his tanned hide was hairless except for a dark patch at the center of his chest.

"Well," he said awkwardly, "what're you doing here?"

"I thought I'd come out and offer a few music lessons—you got any volunteers?"

He squirmed and said, "We thought you'd be in jail."

"You all figure I killed her, huh?"

"I don't—but I thought Orrie did. Grandma said he picked you up."

"Uh-huh. And now you figure I've busted loose and run out here to hide with my friends?"

It was a little unfair to embarrass him like that, but I was sore that he'd taken Ma's advice and faded out when I might have been in serious trouble.

"I know blamed well you wouldn't kill a girl—"

"How about your friends—have you got them convinced?"

"We haven't talked about it," he admitted.

"All right, let's talk about it right now. I want to find out if anybody—you or these others—knows who Flory was going with and why anybody'd want to kill her."

A few minutes later we were sitting in a group on the bank crest. Only a couple of the kids were familiar—when you're in and out of a town as often as I was in Corden, the young ones are hard to keep straight. Somehow they grow so fast and develop so unexpectedly—especially the girls.

The answer to who Flory'd been going with came from Hank.

"She didn't date anybody, at least not when I was

16

around. Nobody called on the telephone or came around. She didn't even get any mail."

I looked at Nancy, Hank's partner. She was greyhound slim with curly brown hair around a bright-eyed fox face. Her blue eyes studied me as though she were planning to paint a portrait from memory. No doubt that was flattering as hell to a kid like Hank but it made me damned uncomfortable.

"What'd you know about her?" I demanded.

"Nothing. None of us'd know much about her—she's been out of school for ages."

"Uh-huh. A whole two years. What're you—a junior this fall?"

She nodded, making her curls bounce.

"Where'd she work before she came to the hotel?"

"At Gus Gardner's Café."

"Waitress?"

"She wasn't the head cook," said Hank. He didn't trust my attention aimed at his girl.

"How come she left there?" I asked Nancy.

"She got fired because she spent too much time flirting with customers."

"Yeah," said Hank, "she was giving Mrs. Gardner too much competition for the guys."

"Oh, Hank," said Nancy in disgust, "she's old." The idea of a woman over thirty being attractive was obscene to her.

Hank claimed he was only kidding and she told him he wasn't one bit funny.

I looked at the other two couples and asked if any of them had been at the dance Saturday night and whether any of them had noticed Flory and who she was with.

The rounder of the two girls said she thought she'd seen Flory dancing with Lard Letnus. I remembered him—he was a little over six feet tall, weighted two-fifteen bare-assed and played fair tackle for Corden High a couple

17

years back. He had a jaw that'd make you believe he could bend railroad spikes with his teeth.

No one had noticed anything else at the dance so I went back to when Flory'd been at the café and didn't get anything more than vague recollections that Lard and several of his old football cronies had hung around the place as long as Flory worked there.

"And when she moved to the hotel, they just dropped her?"

"You'd know as well as I would," said Hank. "You ever see any guys around like that?"

I couldn't quite figure Hank, he was trying to put me on the defensive but the way he went at it made me think he felt vulnerable. I guessed he saw himself as the leader of his group and since they were suspicious of me he had to let them know he was too. I granted that I hadn't noticed any young guys hanging around. A few more questions only made the gap between us more apparent so I got up, thanked them and walked back to my truck. They were still sitting in a tight group, watching me as I backed out of the lot and drove back to town.

I wasn't exactly in a sweet mood when I got back so of course the first thing I saw was Orrie Buford, waddling toward me from City Hall as I climbed down from the truck.

"Where in the Goddamned Billy-blue blazes have you been?" he yelled.

I managed to choke down several smart answers and told him the truth but he was too excited to listen and hollered that I wasn't to leave town again without letting him know by God until this damned killing was settled and did I realize half the town figured I'd cut and run and the other half wanted to lynch him for letting me get away?

I asked if he'd made a house count on that and after some more bright conversation I ambled over to Gus's and took a seat at the counter. Gus wasn't in sight but Rose came over to bring coffee and sympathy. Her face is round, her body bouncy and she gazed at me with mournful brown eyes.

"How you feel, Carl?"

"Gimme a try," I said, shoving my hand across the counter. She put her left hand on mine as she poured coffee with her right and gave me a dimpled smile.

"You're a caution—I thought you'd be hung over something awful."

"Will you hold my head if I am?"

"No."

"That's what I figured. This isn't my popular day."

"Don't you worry, Carl," she assured me, "nobody with any sense believes you hit Flory."

"Yeah, but how many people with sense live in Corden?"

She shook her head and pulled her hand away. When I asked where Gus was she said he never came in early on Sunday. I sipped my coffee and asked if she could tell me who Flory'd been running around with last.

"Huh-uh. Once she left here, I didn't see her at all."

"I thought you were friends."

"Only while she was working here. I never saw her outside of work or after she quit. She was lots younger, you know, we went in different crowds. But I missed her when she quit—she was lots of fun and real sweet. Sometimes she'd get a spell on and say the awfullest things!"

"Like what?"

She giggled and glanced toward the kitchen. "I shouldn't tell you—but like once we were talking about Christ, and somebody said it was tough when ordinary people were supposed to act like Him when here he was, the son of God

19

and all, and Flory said if everybody'd been like Christ there wouldn't be any people because He only came once in over nineteen hundred years. Ain't that awful?"

It was awful enough to make Rose blush and straighten up so she wasn't so close to me.

"I hear lots of guys hung around when Flory was here," I said.

"Lots of guys have always hung around."

"Yeah—but didn't she have her own pack?"

"Yeah," she admitted. "As a matter of fact, almost any guy that came in mostly had eyes for Flory. The most regular ones was Lard and Will Ostrum and a couple others that played football with Lard. He was the steadiest. It wasn't she thought anything special about him, but he sort of buffaloed the others."

"You think he had it bad or was he just hungry?"

"Honey, he was so crazy about that girl he was calf-eyed. It was kinda sad. Flory teased him a lot and made fun of him, behind his back and in front of his face. She said right in front of everybody here that he had a Greek nose and Roman hands and from then on he had to keep his hands in his pockets when he was around her. Everybody laughed and Lard didn't dare get mad because if he showed he was mad she'd just turn him off cold and he couldn't bear that. There was times I really felt sorry for Lard."

I rolled a fresh cigarette and Rose filled my cup again.

"Look," I said, "it's important I know this—do you figure Flory had round heels?"

"No sir. Absolutely not. That girl was way too smart to take chances or be foolish. She didn't drink and she planned to be somebody—don't ever think different. She would've been too."

"Kids told me she was fired—you say she quit. Which was it?"

She sighed, looked uncomfortable and leaned her elbows on the counter.

"She quit—and this is how it was—there was this tableful of fellas, you know, young guys, and she was kidding back and forth with them. I didn't think it was any different than almost any time—we weren't all that rushed—but all of a sudden Gus got mad and said she was here to work, not flirt. He did it right in front of the fellas—I mean he had a regular conniption fit—I never saw him like that before in my life—you know Gus—he's always easygoing and nice as pie. But that night—whew! So, just before she left for home, Flory told Gus she wouldn't be back. She quit, just as flat as that."

"How'd Gus react?"

"Oh, he turned white and stammered some, trying to apologize, I think, and then he said it was up to her and she said it sure was and she walked out."

"Didn't you see her again?"

"No, at least not, you know, person to person. It was sort of like she thought she'd been disgraced and didn't want anything to do with people that'd even seen it happen. Flory was very sensitive, really. I mean, she got all down when anybody acted like she wasn't perfect."

When I started to leave she stopped me.

"You figure on talking to Lard?"

"Yeah, I thought I might."

"You better be careful—he's not one of the people with sense."

"You mean he figures I killed Flory?"

"That's what I've heard. Don't get yourself alone with him. That kid doesn't know his own strength."

"Thanks—I'll keep that in mind."

CHAPTER
3

Corden's the county seat and that summer the only construction I knew of in South Dakota was on our new county courthouse. The money came from state and federal funds, God knows nobody locally had a nickel. Lard worked on the cement crew because his old man knew the contractor. It was Monday noon when I located the muscle boy sitting on a stack of cement sacks, eating from a black lunch bucket. He was tanned copper and his hair was bleached almost white by the sun. Even his eyebrows were pale. His skin was tight over bulging muscles. He squinted up at me when I stopped in front of him and rolled a cigarette.

"I thought you was in jail," he said.

"Not yet. I guess this job keeps you in good shape, eh?"

"I can still lift a sandwich."

I hunkered down and told him straight what I was after. He kept chewing and ignored the other lunching workers who eyed us askance.

When I stopped talking he finished chewing his last bite, wiped his mouth and said, "I'll talk to you tonight. City park. The dugout. Ten o'clock."

"You got yourself a date," I said, and walked off under the stares of the workmen.

Gus still wasn't at the café when I stopped by so I went

22

up the west hill and over a block from Main to Cherry Street where he lived in a white clapboard house with an enclosed porch set on a big corner lot with a garage out back. Gus was in the flower garden beside the garage, pulling weeds.

I gave him the same lead-off I'd used on Lard and he stood there, squinting a little against the sun and nodding. He topped me by about two inches even though he stooped a bit. Black hairs curled in the open V of his khaki shirt and his tanned arms were sinewy and freckled. His face was drawn and his eyes had the glazed look of a man awakened in the middle of the night.

"So what do you expect from me?" he asked in a tired voice.

"Damned if I know, Gus—I'm just trying to feel things out. Why'd Flory leave the café?"

He rubbed soil from his right thumb and stared thoughtfully at the daisy patch on his right. "I guess she got sick of waiting on tables."

"Was she good at the job?"

He lifted his head in a nervous jerk and peered at me. Deep creases ran from his nose to his mouth, giving him a pained look. He swallowed.

"Yes. Most of the time. She wasn't as steady as Rose but when her spirits were good she worked very hard because she liked people and wanted them to love her. Anybody she waited on felt important. And more than that, the people she worked with liked her. It wasn't just because she was pretty and good-natured—but you felt she was vulnerable. If she got so much as a hint that somebody was unhappy with her, she just folded up, like a delicate flower touched by frost—"

"Yeah—I heard she couldn't take criticism."

"That wasn't it at all," he said angrily. "You could correct Flory—she accepted criticism beautifully—if you

23

didn't make her think it was personal. If she thought you were angry with her, or even impatient, well, that just destroyed her. When something horrible happens to a girl like Flory—you have to feel such awful guilt—"

"You figure if she hadn't left your place, she might be okay?"

He shook his head and waved his hand impatiently. "No—no—of course not. It could've happened in back of the café as easily as behind the hotel—that's too obvious to talk about. It's just that I wish I'd treated her more as an understanding father—"

"How did you treat her?"

He glanced toward the house before meeting my eye.

"I leaned over backward because Flory was too easy to like. I felt she needed discipline—she was too used to having everyone tell her how wonderful she was. I was afraid she'd be spoiled."

"So she quit after you got tough once too often, huh?"

His eyes slipped away from me again and turned toward the house. "I don't remember, really. One day she quit and that was it. You'll have to excuse me now, I don't feel well, I'm going in to rest."

I watched him all the way to the house. He walked with great effort, as though the level yard were a steep hill.

That night was clear and still. I walked through the young trees planted in rows along the southwest corner of the city park until I came to the softball diamond on the northeast corner. The dugout was only a low shelter over a long bench flanking the first-base path. It wasn't ten yet so I wasn't surprised that Lard hadn't shown and I rolled a cigarette and lit it while leaning against the shelter roof. There was no moon but the stars were bright enough to expose the ball field with its pale base paths and the low pitcher's mound in the center. A screen door slammed in a house to the north and somebody called a dog.

I was through the cigarette and thinking of another when I sighted Lard coming through the trees. He walked neither fast nor slow, like a man going to work at a job he didn't enjoy. When he reached the dugout he didn't look at me directly, just nodded and squinted around in every direction. I thought of Rose's warning against meeting him alone.

No one was in sight and there were lights in only two of the houses facing the park. Lard fished a pack of cigarettes from his shirt pocket as he ducked under the shelter roof and sat down on the bench inside. I joined him.

"Haven't you heard those'll cut your wind?" I asked.

"Horseshit."

"By golly, I never thought of it quite like that—you really get to the guts of a question, don't you?"

He dropped his match, stepped on it and leaned his elbows on his knees.

"What'd you tell Orrie to make him let you go free?" he demanded.

"I told him I didn't do it—so what didn't you want to talk about in the daylight?"

He sat back and stared at the glowing tip of the cigarette in his big fist.

"I figure only a nut would've killed Flory. Somebody drunk and horny and no Goddamned good." He turned his thick head and looked at me.

"That's one notion," I granted. "Can you tell me why she left Gus's Café—and how come she stopped seeing guys once she made the move to the hotel?"

He took a deep drag on the cigarette. "She left Gus's because she was sore at me. She told me not to come around but of course she couldn't make me not and so she quit. And she didn't see guys at the hotel because nobody wanted to buck your old lady."

"You telling me Ma scared you off?"

"Nobody scares me off of nothing. I laid off because Flory was mad and I was afraid she'd leave town if I pushed too hard."

"What was she mad about?"

"I offered to bust Will Ostrum's nose if he didn't stay clear. She didn't like me spooking other guys—Flory liked lots of company. I was pretty dumb because she didn't really give a damn about Will—it was the principle of the thing. She said I didn't own her."

"But when she left Gus's, she didn't go with any other guys—doesn't that seem funny to you?"

"Naw. Who was she gonna meet at the hotel? Just you and your old man, your punk nephew—hell, she was just coasting. She wouldn't have stayed there long."

"Guys come to the hotel. A salesman tried to get her to go for a ride with him about a week ago. Sharp dude with a brand new Chevy."

"What'd she say?"

"She said she didn't care for wrestling."

"Yeah"—he nodded—"that was Flory's style. The guy leave it at that?"

"Salesmen never leave anything anywhere. He kept trying until Flory got up and walked out."

"Was the guy mad?"

"No. Like he told me before he went down to the movie alone, if you don't ask, you'll never know."

"You ask?"

If you've got to ask you never get it but I figured this wasn't the time for deep philosophy.

"Flory was a little young for me."

"That ain't the way I hear it—I hear if they're big enough, they're old enough for Carl Wilcox."

"You listen to a lot of crap."

He dropped his cigarette, ground it into the dust under his feet and stepped clear of the dugout. Again he looked all around. One of the lights across the street had gone out. He scowled down at me.

"I figure you killed Flory. You were drunk and you tried to get her to lay down and she wouldn't so you got mad and hit her. Now let's just quit farting around and you tell the truth. You killed her and I'm gonna make you admit it."

"What kind of sense does that make?" I asked. I was trying to sound relaxed but it didn't sound convincing even to me. He looked ten feet tall and wide as Texas looming over me. "You think if I do say it was me to keep from having my head wind up like Flory's—then we're gonna go down to City Hall and I'll sign a confession in front of Orrie and that'll be it?"

He wasn't in a debating mood. He snatched at my foot and was some surprised to catch it on the jaw instead of in his hand. It staggered him but he still managed to grab my leg and I had to roll hard to jerk free and come up facing him in a crouch.

"Don't be a damned fool—" I began as he charged. I slipped aside and tried to kick his feet out from under him but only managed to trip us both and again we came up about a yard apart. "Damnit, Lard, cut it out—you're too damned big to fool with—"

I skipped to the right when he rushed and caught him with a kidney punch that should have made him sick for a week. Instead of folding he grunted and swung a backhand that clipped my noggin just over the ear and knocked me ass over teakettle.

That did it. I came up throwing knuckles and for several seconds he got speared, clipped, hooked, jabbed and clubbed. He went down the first time more from confusion than real damage. I let him get to his knees and uncorked my Sunday punch which planted him flat on his back. For several seconds he lay there, wheezing. Then, very slowly, he rolled over and managed to climb up on his knees and elbows. He kept his head down.

"You try to get up again," I told him, "and I'll boot your teeth out. We're through playing around."

He spat blood on the dust, shook his head and said, "I believe it."

"And you can believe I didn't kill Flory. Why the hell do I think I'd have to take a club to her?"

He shook his head, tried to settle down on his hip and tumbled over like a tipped turtle. After a while he sat up and touched his mouth with his right hand.

"I got a loose tooth."

"You're damned lucky it's only one."

He nodded and took a deep, tortured breath. "Jesus. I never seen anybody so fast. It ain't fair."

"It is so, I'm littler. Listen, was Flory interested in any other guys you knew about?"

He sighed, spit blood and wiped his mouth carefully.

"She liked 'em all—but nobody special—not even me."

"Was it like that from the start?"

He took another deep breath, gazed across the softball field and shook his head. "No. About the third time I walked her home—that was last fall—I thought she liked me special. I'd given her a little box of candy—she liked that. She liked any kind of present. Anyway, she got talking about what she was gonna do. She was gonna get enough money and go to the Cities and from there she was going to California. She had it all planned. She didn't say she was gonna get in movies but I knew even then that was what she figured on. So I told her I was gonna be a football star—go to the University of Minnesota. She got excited about that. She kissed me. Real good. Nobody ever kissed like Flory."

28

"So what happened then?"

"What the hell do you mean, what happened? She kissed me, I told you."

"I mean after that night. When'd she start acting the same toward you as other guys?"

"Oh—it was just never that good again. The Saturday after that we played Fabin High and they beat the hell out of us. I got my nose broke in the third quarter and didn't see her for over a week and it was never the same. When I asked about her plans after that she didn't want to talk about them."

Flory, obviously, was not sold on losers.

"I figure it was because I was a year behind her in school. She was only a few months older but she graduated a year before me. Girls are funny about stuff like that."

"Uh-huh. Rose tells me Flory quit Gus because he bawled her out in front of a crowd. Gus says she quit because she was tired of waiting on tables. You really think she left there because of you?"

He shook his head woefully. "No. Rose is right. Flory wouldn't take any shit. She always did just what she wanted. I heard Gus blew his stack and that'd do it for sure. Before that time he let her get away with anything—she even left without cleaning up the joint more than once. Old Joel always took care of things for her and Gus knew it and let him."

"Was Joel sweet on Flory too?"

"Hell yes, everybody was sweet on Flory."

"No," I said, "somebody wasn't sweet on her at all."

"I guess not—but it hadda be somebody crazy. If it wasn't you, it was some other nut."

I left him sitting on the ground gingerly feeling his loose tooth.

• CHAPTER
4

The hotel was dead quiet and mostly dark when I got back. I climbed the creaking stairs and walked down the empty, shadowed hall, passed my room and Hank's, opened the door beyond, stepped inside and groped a second before finding the string that pulled on the overhead light.

This was where Flory had slept each night during the last few months of her life. It had blue and white striped wallpaper, a white ceiling and blue curtains. When she woke in the morning and sat up with her feet on the bare floor, Flory could look out the east window and catch a clear view of the graveled street below, Craven's gas station across the way and the dark side of Amundson's Hall beyond. Without getting up she could reach the commode drawers and pick her underwear for the day. On the wall, over the commode, was a slightly crooked mirror lined with snapshots of herself taken on bright summer days. Immediately left of the commode was a white, straight-backed chair with a laundry bag on the seat and a pink sweater draped over the back. Half a dozen dresses drooped from hangers on hooks along the west wall behind the door and a blue bathrobe dangled from the door hook. High-heeled shoes, one pair black, the other white and black, stood gleaming primly with their heels to the wall. A pair of brown work shoes had been shoved under the foot of the bed. I sat down on the tasseled white spread, reached over to the chair and pulled the laundry bag over beside me. It held a few pairs of silk stockings and some pink underwear.

I opened the top drawer of the commode and found it filled with underwear, stockings and hankies, all neatly folded and packed in correct piles. The things on top were ordinary pink and white, but underneath there were black and red affairs with lace. The stockings on top were everyday shades, underneath they were black and spiderweb sheer.

The smaller drawers held her makeup and beauty stuff, toilet waters and cologne and two small, very fancy bottles of expensive perfume. Under a package of sanitary napkins I found a black leather case filled with silverplated manicure tools set in red velvet.

I found movie magazines piled nearly a foot high behind the commode door and on top of the stack there was a box filled with pages torn from other magazines. Her favorites had been Clark Gable and Jean Harlow but she was also strong on Ronald Colman, Charles Boyer and Robert Montgomery. At the bottom of the box I found an autographed eight-by-ten glossy of Gable.

There were no pictures of girl or boyfriends, no letters or cards, old programs or souvenirs, nothing at all to suggest a personal relationship except for the obvious gift items.

I was still sitting on the bed, thinking of how barren and unsentimental Flory's world appeared in this nun's cell, when a creak down the hall caught my ear.

I stood up, jerked the light cord and stepped over to the wall behind the curtain. My back brushed against the dresses which were faintly scented with cologne. Someone moved down the hall toward me, like a ponderous cat, and halted outside the door. I froze against the wall. The door handle rattled gently, turned and suddenly pale light from the hall fell into the room and across the white bedspread. I saw a gun, extended into the room, then withdrawn quickly.

"Awright—I know you're back of the door—just move slow with your hands up and come in sight before you get hurt."

"Oh, for Christ's sake," I said, and stepped into the center of the room to pull the light cord.

Orrie stood in the hall, blinking stupidly, but the gun stayed level on my gut.

"What in the hell do you think you're doing?" he demanded.

"Right now I'm wishing you'd point that Goddamned cannon at the floor—or better yet, put it away."

He grunted, flipped on the safety and jammed the thing into his holster.

"I seen the light from the street—knew it was Flory's room—figured I'd check. So what're you doing in here?"

I sat back down on the bed.

"I was going through the effects of the deceased—which I suppose you've already done?"

"Yup." He shoved the laundry bag off the chair and sat down facing me.

"Did you take away some jewelry?"

He grinned. "You don't miss much, do you? Yeah, there was a little basket kind of box, full of stuff. I took it over to Winkler's Jewelry to see if any of it was worth anything. It wasn't."

"How about letters or a diary—?"

"Nothing like that."

"So all she was was neat, huh?"

"Even the stuff in the laundry bag was good as clean."

"I don't think she bought the manicure set herself."

"I don't imagine—nor the fancy underwear and silk

32

stockings. There's nothing like that in Corden. Did you know her ma?"

"Should I?"

"I wouldn't be surprised—you know most of the women in this town. Lives up the hill, a ways south, a widow woman in a shack. Old man ran off about seven–eight years ago. Died in a train wreck out west. Flory left her ma the day she finished high school and got work. Hasn't been back since."

"Well," I said, "you can be damned sure whoever gave her the presents had more money than Lard or me."

"So what? It didn't have to be her lover that did her in— it could've been somebody jealous or a drunk with a hard-on—"

"You figure that was the murder weapon? That'd be a dilly—"

"You're damned near funny as a boil on the ass," he said, getting up. "Just remember, you ain't clear of this yet—I'll be around tomorrow—you be here."

"I can hardly wait."

CHAPTER
5

Bertha was in a mood when I came down to the kitchen on Tuesday morning but it didn't hurt her cooking any. She laid out two eggs with crisp bacon, golden toast and grape jam. The coffee was steaming and stout.

After eating I took a second cup, tilted my chair back and squinted at Bertha. Her gray-streaked hair was pulled back into a big bun, her red cheeks glistened like polished apples and her wide mouth was tight as a corset string on the preacher's wife.

"What'd Flory do nights?" I asked.

"How the hell would I know? I suppose she slept, like everybody else except maybe you."

"She never gabbed about fellas or movies or *anything*?"

"In this kitchen, we work, we don't gab."

"Are you telling me that kid never spoke a word to you?"

Her tight mouth cracked a little, then opened in a grin. She had fine teeth, whiter than goat's milk.

"I do remember her asking about you once. She wanted to know if you ever managed to rob a place and get away. All she ever heard was about you getting caught."

"What'd you say?"

"I said the only thing you was good at was getting into girls' pants. I told her to watch out."

"That was damned Christian of you. No wonder she was skittier than a spooked colt around me."

"What I said wouldn't matter to her—she was too smart to fall for any of your guff."

"How'd you figure that if she never talked?"

"It ain't what they say that makes me know when people are smart—it's what they do."

I thanked her for being helpful as a broken crutch and moseyed out to the lobby office as Elihu came out of the bedroom across the hall. His fine white hair was a tangle, one suspender was twisted and his shirt was open at the collar, showing his gray underwear top.

"Well," he said, giving me his church-elder scowl, "you just coming in from a night on the town?"

"No—Bertha and I've been holding prayer services out in the kitchen—putting in a word for you."

He grunted and pawed at his white hair. "I got a tintype of that, all right—you gonna drive over to Franton and pick up that boiler for me today?"

"You'll have to ask Orrie—he's ordered me to stay in town."

"Well, shitfire—couldn't you stay out of trouble for just twenty-four hours once?"

"I don't know—I might try when I get as old as you."

He shook his head and clumped out toward the kitchen.

I'd hardly settled down in his swivel chair and started building a smoke when Orrie Buford shoved his way in the front door, looked all around and sat down on a rocker facing me. It complained loudly as he leaned back.

"You're up early," I said.

"Can't sleep. Is Hank up?"

"Don't make me laugh, it's not even eight yet."

"Well, roust him out—I wanta talk with him."

"When you wanted to talk with me you came and

damned near pounded the door down—why this delicate approach for Hank?"

"He ain't a prime suspect—but I know he's a smart kid and he might've noticed something."

I went upstairs after Hank, knowing the big difference was that Ma doted on her grandson and had written me off. At the same time my opinion of Orrie rose a notch because he was shrewd enough to know Hank was sharp.

After a quick knock I opened the door and stuck my head into Hank's room. He had the green shade drawn tight and the room was dark and warm as a womb. I walked between the bed and bureau, let the shade up and considered the body buried under the covers and pillow.

"The law's downstairs," I said, "come down and face the music."

The pillow slowly moved aside and Hank peered up at me.

"How come you're up?" It was an accusation.

"I didn't want to miss anything—like you getting the third degree. Shag ass downstairs—Orrie Buford's waiting with handcuffs in one hand and a rubber hose in the other."

His eyes widened more than I'd have expected from anybody so sleepy and innocent and the next second he was up, scrambling into his clothes.

"Why me?" he muttered.

"You'll see."

We went down the stairs together and walked into the lobby.

"Some of us," said Orrie without rising, "ain't so easy about what happened that we can sleep all morning."

That seemed too farfetched to reach Hank, but to my surprise, it did. He looked worried and even guilty as he sat down in a rocker across from Orrie.

"Now," said the cop, "just how well did you know Flory?"

Hank stared at him, glanced briefly at me and took a deep breath.

"I didn't know her hardly at all."

"No? You lived under the same roof with a knockout of a young lady and you didn't get to know her at all in half a summer?"

"Well, she was four years older than me—what'd we talk about?"

Orrie gave me an exasperated look, as if I were responsible for my nephew's answers, and turned back to ask if he'd noticed any fellows of Flory's advanced age hanging around the hotel.

"Grandma doesn't allow fellows to hang around here."

"Geez," said Orrie, "I keep forgetting this is a convent. Okay—so did you ever see her with fellows outside these sacred walls?"

"Not this summer—until Saturday night."

"You saw her Saturday, over at the dance hall?"

"Yeah."

"You dance with her?"

"Saturday?"

"Anytime, Goddamnit."

Hank looked painfully embarrassed—at least I thought it was embarrassment—I wasn't too sure—and finally admitted he had danced with her last summer. "I didn't know how old she was—she was small—you know? I figured she was my age."

"Okay. You danced with her—what'd you talk about?"

"Well, gee, that was a whole year ago—the usual stuff—like what a swell dancer she was and how pretty. What you tell a girl."

"How'd she like it?"

"She smiled a lot."

"You dance with her more than once?"

Hank looked at me and I winked. It didn't encourage him any. He looked at the floor and said, "Yeah—I guess maybe two or three times."

"Three times? A girl dances with a fella three times around here, she usually lets him walk her home. Did you walk Flory home?"

Hank's face turned red as he nodded.

Orrie's chair creaked as he leaned forward, squinting. "You kiss her?"

"No."

"You sure?"

Hank's head came up and he scowled. "Of course I'm sure—you think I wouldn't remember that?"

"You try?"

"No."

"Always try," I told him, "it beats wishing you had later."

"Yeah, I can see that."

"Goddamnit!" yelled Orrie, "I'm questioning a man, keep your Goddamned romantic advice for later."

"Yessir," I said and when I winked at Hank this time he grinned.

"Okay," said Orrie, lowering his voice, "so now we know you was interested in Flory last summer even if she was an old woman. You see her again after that night you walked her home?"

"No. I went back home with my folks to North Dakota the next day."

"So what'd you do when you got here this summer and found her working in the hotel?"

He shrugged. "By then I knew she was a lot older than me—I figured she wouldn't be interested."

"Uh-huh. But that didn't keep you from making a little

try—did it? You talked to her—ever ask why she never went over to the dance hall anymore?"

He turned red again. "I offered to pay her way if she'd go with me."

"What'd she say?"

"She said thanks, but people might think she was robbing the cradle."

"When'd this happen?"

"The first week after I got here in June."

"How'd you feel about what she said—did it make you mad?"

Hank took a deep breath and frowned as he let it out.

"No, it was true—why should I get mad?"

Orrie settled back in the creaking chair. "Son, there ain't nothing like the truth to upset a man sometimes. Not when it comes from a pretty girl."

"I didn't kill her," said Hank in a tight voice.

"I never suspicioned it," said Orrie as he folded his fat hands across his paunch. "Not for a second. But I wanted to know how Flory handled fellas. It sounds like she could easy say the wrong thing to the wrong one. Okay—you just run along now—you must be hungry for breakfast."

Still scowling, Hank got up and walked slowly out toward the kitchen.

"Ain't that something?" said Orrie when we were alone. "A year ago that girl would've told Hank she couldn't go out with him because his grandma'd be mad at her. She might've believed what she said but before this year she wanted all the guys panting and she didn't ever turn off a fella permanent. I just don't get it one Goddamned bit."

"Maybe she was growing up."

He shook his head. "Gals don't grow up in that direction."

Elihu walked in from the hall, took a cigar from the counter case beside the register desk and glowered at me

39

while he lit up. If Orrie hadn't been there I'd have sat tight until the old man was riled enough to rumble but I don't believe in starting family rows in front of outsiders so I slid out of the throne and sat on a rocker beside Orrie. Elihu moved in, took his proper place and gazed out on his kingdom.

"I suppose," he said to Orrie, "you got this whole killing all figured out by now?"

"No," said Orrie, shaking his head. "There ain't nothing simple about this case."

Elihu turned his cigar in his dry fingers and nodded. He had combed his white hair smooth and buttoned his shirt but the suspender was still twisted and would stay that way until Ma came out and spotted him.

"How about that football fella—Lard—I hear he was sweet on her and he's a hothead—?"

"His folks claim he was home in bed when it happened."

"Huh! Lots of folks think their young'uns are home in bed when they're not." He turned his head to give me a long, significant look.

"Mebbe—but I got no proof otherwise. You or the Mrs. ever notice any other fellas around?"

"She didn't even get a phone call that I know of. Blamed funny—she was a damned fine-looking girl."

"I think she had a man she couldn't be seen with," I said.

They both turned to stare at me.

"Like who?" asked Orrie.

"Try Gus."

Orrie snorted in disgust. "He's too damned old—besides—from all I hear—they hardly talked except when he got mad and yelled at her."

"That's one of the things that makes me wonder. Gus is everybody's favorite uncle—father confessor—how come with this pretty girl he was all business? How come she's the only one he ever lost his temper with?"

Orrie still looked unconvinced and I reminded him that someone had been giving Flory presents. "She was ambitious and smart—she wanted out of Corden. Who else with money did she ever meet?"

"Where'd you get the notion she was so ambitious?"

I asked if he'd talked with Lard.

"Yeah, I did—and he mostly told me you was the likeliest killer suspect. Matter of fact he about let me know if I didn't pin it on you he'd handle matters himself. You'd best keep out of his way—that's one fella I don't figure you can handle."

My grin slipped out before I could swallow it and he glared at me.

"Don't take that as a dare, Goddamnit—stay out of his way."

"You seen him this morning?"

"No—why?"

"He invited me to the park last night."

His eyes lifted to the ceiling. "What happened?"

"Well, I learned a few things—like she lost interest in him when she found he was a loser, cut him dead for scaring off other fellas, and she was making big plans for herself. I also found out that Lard's not what you'd call cat quick."

Orrie tipped the rocker forward, came to his feet and started for the door. "Don't go anyplace," he threw at me as he went out, "I'll be right back and I want you here."

Elihu glared at me as Orrie huffed down the street and said, "I suppose this means you won't be able to pick up that boiler for me today."

"That's what makes you so lovable," I told him, "you never lose sight of what's most important in this world."

Orrie was back in less than an hour, shaking his head

and glowering at me so ferociously it must have given him a headache.

"You're a Goddamned caution, Wilcox—I'd ought to lock you up for assault and battery—attacking a boy like that!"

"If I'd attacked that gorilla, I'd ask to be committed. And if that's the picture you got, why didn't Lard swear out a warrant for my arrest?"

"I'm damned if I know why—but he won't. Did you really kick him in the jaw?"

"I just nudged him a little when he grabbed for my leg."

"He looks like you stomped the living Jesus out of him."

"Is that what he claims?"

"No," he admitted grudgingly, "he says most of it was, fists—were you carrying a rock?"

"No—but there might've been a little sand in my finger-nails—"

He shook his head. "Somebody's gonna take you one of these days—I hope I live to see it."

"Now there's a noble ambition—I appreciate that, Orrie."

He got up, walked to the door and glared at the heat waves shimmering over the graveled street. "One thing," he said, "you seem to have clubbed Lard out of the notion it was you that killed Flory. He couldn't tell me just why, but he's convinced."

"When a man whips you fair and square, Orrie, you don't like to figure he's a villain."

"Uh-huh. I'll promise you this—I ain't ever gonna let that happen to me. I don't ever plan to start ignoring facts. I'll see you later."

CHAPTER
6

Thunder woke me at five A.M. and I lay on my back, listening to the rumble as I watched lightning flash through the blind, turning the room white for seconds at a time. Then the wind came, moaning low before it sharpened to a whistle and dropped spattering rain on the roof. When it blows that hard, water works through places everywhere in the hotel: the roof, around window casings and even through the walls. Long dry spells with hot winds shrink wood until we're lucky the walls don't look like a corn-crib side.

In fifteen minutes it had moved off, muttering toward the southeast. Most of the storms were like that in South Dakota in the early thirties—hit, raise hell and run, like a Viking raid. They dumped water all in a bunch, raced across the land to low spots, carrying topsoil and leaving nothing but gullies that were dry before noon and dusty by sundown. At least this time there'd been no hail.

I loaded trash on the truck after breakfast and hauled it out to the dump since that was along the way to pick up the boiler Elihu had been nagging me about.

It irritated me some that a few feisty rats were running around while I was dumping the load and as soon as I got the truck bed clear I decided to get my slingshot and teach them why old rats stayed out of sight through the day.

My emergency blanket is always in a roll on top of my

43

toolbox behind the driver's seat and when I moved it something felt strange and I rolled the blanket open. The thing stuck to the wool and even before I shook it loose I knew what I was going to find.

The morning rain had left the day fairly cool, but I sat down on the running board and felt sweat trickling down from my temples and armpits. What would Orrie do if I brought him the murder weapon and told him where I'd found it? I figured he'd grab his first clue and slap me in the hoosegow—partly because he'd be mad that I'd produced it from my truck which had been only a few yards away from the corpse; a fact which would make some folks figure he'd been sloppy for not searching. I wasn't too sure he wouldn't claim he'd found it himself.

After a while I climbed back in the truck, drove to town and parked in the alley behind Doc Feeney's office. Then I telephoned Orrie from Doc's phone. Orrie claimed he was busy but agreed to come over when I told him I'd found something important. When he showed up I led Doc and him down to the truck and asked Doc to look behind the seat and check out the blanket there. He gave me a fussy-annoyed look but was too nosy to argue and a second later I heard him gasp.

"What is it?" demanded Orrie.

"Take a look."

A minute later the three of us were up in Doc's office with the blanket on his examining table, looking at a length of iron pipe about fifteen by one and a half inches and covered with stains that had made it stick to the blanket.

"Where'd you find that?" Orrie asked.

I told him about my dump-ground trip.

"That your blanket?"

"Sure thing."

"How about the pipe?"

44

"I wasn't carrying it. Hell, I'm no plumber and I don't need a club."

"So where'd it come from?"

"Well, I don't believe in the tooth fairy so I'd guess it was stuck in there by the murderer. He probably lifted it from the trash pile beside the garage."

"I looked in that pile—there wasn't any pipe there."

"That figures—this length is about all Elihu'd waste."

He didn't argue that—nobody who knew Elihu would. Orrie turned to Doc who assured him the pipe matched the diameter he figured for the murder weapon.

"Listen," I said, "I've got a notion."

Orrie took his eyes from the bloodstained pipe and squinted at me suspiciously. "About what?"

"Whoever planted that pipe must be dying to get you looking for it—sooner or later he's got to tip you off. So we just keep quiet about finding it and see where the tip comes from."

Doc brushed his glossy beard with his fingers and thumb, Orrie just looked fat and miserable.

"He makes sense," said Doc.

"And what if Carl takes off while I'm waiting around?"

"Hell, Orrie," I said, "if I was gonna take off I'd have done it when I found the pipe. Why show it to you and then skip?"

"Damned if I know—but you done some pretty God-damned strange things in your time, Carl."

"Sober?"

"Maybe not—but you never been sober long."

I didn't have a comeback for that cheap shot and let it pass. Doc took some scrapings from the pipe before turning it over to Orrie for hiding and I took my blanket back to the truck and drove to Franton for Elihu's boiler.

CHAPTER
7

Hank stopped me as I was coming out of the washroom just before supper. His wavy black hair flopped over his forehead and a deep scowl brought his eyebrows so low he could hardly eyeball me without tilting his head back.

"Uncle Carl, did Orrie mean it when he said he never suspected me?"

"Probably. He hasn't got much imagination."

He flushed and glared at me. "What's that supposed to mean?"

"It means I figure you handed him a line of thin crap."

"You think *I* killed her?"

"Nope. But you sure as hell weren't as standoffish as you tried to make him think."

Hank glanced toward the dining-room door and then looked me in the eye. "I've got to talk with you."

"Fine, I can work you in right after I put on the feed bag—come up to my room."

He was so antsy I found him in my room when I went upstairs after stuffing down Bertha's pork chops, mashed potatoes and gravy, beet greens and apple pie.

Hank sat on the straight chair beside my bureau and I plunked down on the bed and started rolling a cigarette.

"Listen," he said, "you're going to have to solve this murder."

"Me? What're folks paying a town cop for?"

"To lock up drunks and direct traffic Saturday nights. He doesn't know anything about solving murders."

"So what qualifies me?"

"You've been in prison—you know how the criminal mind works—I mean—you've lived with people like that. Didn't you know any murderers in prison?"

"Not a one. The fact is, every man in stir is innocent. I was the only man in the whole joint who ever admitted doing anything."

"You always kid about everything," he complained. "This is really serious. I think Orrie was lying when he said he didn't suspect me—I think he figures I had something to do with it—"

"How the hell could someone 'have something to do' with beating a girl's brains out?"

He shook his head impatiently. "I *was* interested in Flory. I even wrote letters to her—"

"So you lied about her not getting any mail?"

"Mine didn't count. Flory picked up the mail every day until I came in June and from then on I got it and she never got any mail all that time." He wanted to convince himself even more than me that he had put no blot on the family honor and he kept looking me in the eye so we'd know he was honest.

I stared back at him until finally he looked at the floor a moment, took a deep breath and let it out.

"What's important," he said, looking at me again, "is that I came here for Easter vacation. I knew she was working at the hotel and I wanted to see her and be around—"

"Uh-huh. So what happened?"

"Nothing, really. I helped her make beds one morning and drank a lot of coffee in the kitchen, took a lot of guff from Bertha and finally asked Flory to go to the Wednesday

47

night Old Time dance with me. She said Grandma wouldn't approve and what's more, she said not to come up and help her make beds because it'd get her fired."

"She was damned right. None of your Puritans'll ever believe a couple can be in a room with a bed and not use it. Okay, so you wooed and lost, and you tried again this summer and she cut you down with the cradle-robbing crack. So where were you Saturday night?"

Hank stood up, went to the window and looked down at the drive out back. "I heard from Tim Waddell that Flory had gone to the dance. I didn't want to see her there with other guys hanging around, so I took a walk. I hiked along the railroad tracks west, clear to the bend at the top of the hill and on around—"

"Just you and the stars, huh?"

"That's right. I didn't see anybody. I walked back late— it was nearly two. I even cut through the back of the hotel—Flory had to be laying there, dead, under the trees. I must've passed within twenty feet of her—"

"Jesus Christ," I said.

"Yeah," he agreed, and came back to sit down and look miserable. "So you see why you've got to figure this thing out. I can help."

"That'll make it easy."

He looked at me reproachfully. "This isn't anything to clown about."

"All right, you've given it some thought—what ideas have you got?"

"Well, I read a mystery once where a guy was killed by a girl who wanted to get her boyfriend in trouble. I mean, she had to get rid of this fellow who looked like he was going to keep her from marrying a rich guy."

"Why kill the other fella?"

"It was kind of complicated—but there was no motive anybody could see for *her* to kill the guy—but there *was*

48

for her boyfriend. She framed him, see? So maybe somebody with nothing against Flory figured he could kill her and everybody'd think you did it. Just like they do."

"That's too damned farfetched—and not everybody thinks I did it."

"Well, a lot do. If that's how it is, somebody'll plant evidence on you to strengthen the case, see?"

That was way too close to seem coincidental and I found myself staring at him suspiciously before I reminded myself of his sterling purity and shook it off.

"I suppose I'd ought to be flattered," I said, "that you figure someone thinks I'm important enough for so much attention—but between us fellas, I can't think of anybody that takes Carl Wilcox that seriously."

"Oh, there must be lots of guys—"

I don't consider myself thin-skinned but he said that with more assurance than I found tasteful and I asked, a little testy, "Like who?"

"Just about every stuffed shirt in town—take Judge Segal, and Mayor Tenneson—and all the guys you've pulled practical jokes on—old Harcourt and Davies—the two you talked into fighting each other—all the guys you whipped at Lake Kampie and in back of the dance hall—"

"I have some trouble picturing old Judge Segal out in back of the hotel swinging a club—and almost as much thinking of Tenneson in that spot."

"Well," he said, flipping his hand casually, "I was just illustrating that there are people around sore at you. Besides—they could hire somebody to do the dirty work."

"Hank, people in Corden don't have the dough or connections to hire killers."

"Okay—how about Nate? I bet he'd do it just for spite."

That made enough sense to give me a chill. Nate was the oldest son of my onetime sweetheart, Jenny Larson. I'd whipped his ass after he belted me without warning in his

49

ma's kitchen about two years back. It'd wrecked my romance with Jenny and that was what Nate wanted.

"Naw," I said, after a second's thought, "he's not even living in town anymore. He works in Loden, at the creamery."

"That's only twenty miles away."

I put my cigarette out and thought on that some. Nate sure as hell had no love for me—and the tricky stunt was his specialty.

"No"—I shook my head—"it's too damned farfetched."

"Well, I'll find out where he was that night, just in case."

After dark I wandered north toward Jenny's house which was about five blocks from downtown. Another of the elms lining the south side of her lot had died since my last visit and I wondered if every tree in Corden wouldn't wither away in the sun before winter.

A little light came through the front windows overlooking the porch as I ambled up the front walk and I guessed it came from the kitchen in back where Jenny spent most of her time, cooking, ironing, washing, canning and in my regular visiting days, making beer about once a month. I started around the north side and walked over the parched lawn. On my right was the graveled driveway where Joe, her long-dead sign-painter husband, had used to park his Model T when he came home from road trips.

I stopped at the shed behind the kitchen and rapped gently on the screen door. A second later she stood, silhouetted against the light, looking down at me.

"Hi," I said, "how've you been?"

"It doesn't matter to you how I've been—that's none of your concern."

"Then what am I doing here?"

"I can't imagine. I'm engaged, you know. I've got a ring."

She waved her left hand at me. "I don't want you coming around, making talk and trouble."

"A little talk's no trouble, Jenny, it's civil."

"You aren't civilized enough to be civil to. Go away."

"How's Nate?"

"Just fine—no thanks to you."

"He come around to visit his ma now and then?"

She tilted her head. "Why'd you want to know that?"

"It seems he should, that's all—but I haven't seen him around town in quite a while."

"Well, don't concern yourself."

"Okay, so he hasn't been around."

"He has so. Had dinner with us Saturday. Does that relieve you?"

It didn't. It made me sorry I'd asked. So I lied.

"Yeah, some. Did he stay over?"

"Why should he? He's got his own place now—went back to Loden after the dance—in his car he bought."

"My, working steady sets a man up, doesn't it?"

"You must've learned that from observation—you sure haven't had the experience."

I grinned at her. "You know, the way you love to slap me down—I sure wonder how you can stay happy with a fella like your salesman. What in the world can you have fun digging him about?"

"Bill doesn't need any digging. He's fine and honest and considerate—and he's fun, too."

She was so earnest I felt like a rat for asking questions that were really meant to get her son for murder. So he *was* a prick—Jenny was about the finest woman I'd ever met.

"Jenny," I told her, "I hope you're gonna be happy as hell. Good night."

And I turned around and went back to the hotel.

CHAPTER
8

"**N**ate was at the dance last Saturday night," Hank told me the next morning. I was sitting in the lobby having an after-breakfast smoke while Elihu was out in the kitchen filling his face.

"Alone?"

"I guess so. He asked Nancy for a dance but she turned him down because he was drunk."

"Any word on how late he stayed?"

"Till the last dog was hung, from what I hear."

"Anybody see him after the dance?"

"I don't know—I'll check around—"

Just before noon I was parked in a wooden chair outside the hotel front when a Norseland Dairy truck wheeled by and I spotted Nate in the passenger's seat. It seemed like too much of a coincidence for nature but when I got up and went to the corner I could see the truck parking in front of Gus's and sure enough, Nate climbed down from the cab and walked inside with the driver.

Nate's rat eyes spotted me the moment I walked into the café. He had a wide mouth, a narrow nose, lots of forehead and curly hair that was the envy of every girl in Corden. The man with him was fat and dark—I guessed part Indian. His puffy cheeks were so high they crowded his dark eyes, giving him a permanent smiley look.

I hung one cheek on the nearest counter stool and smiled down at them.

"Long time no see."

Nate grinned, friendlier than a wagged tail.

"Well," he said, "you out on parole?"

I grinned back. "If I was, I wouldn't dare come around you. Parolees got to be careful who they're seen with."

Nate tipped his head toward his fat companion and jerked a thumb at me. "You wouldn't believe it—but this fella's even faster with his hands than with his mouth."

"I hear you had dinner with your ma Saturday," I said.

"Yeah? Where'd you hear that?"

"Your ma told me."

"Come on—Ma's engaged—why'd she talk to you?"

"Engaged women can still talk to other fellas."

He shook his head solemnly. "Not fellas like you, Wilcox. Not if they're smart."

"Yeah," I admitted, "she saw it the same way. But last Saturday was so special, people just can't help talking about it to almost anybody. You came to visit, Flory came out of hiding and went to a dance and got herself murdered—I suppose you heard about that?"

He looked pleasantly thoughtful. "Seems I did—fact is— that's one of the reasons I was so surprised to see you still on the loose. Didn't she work in your old man's hotel?"

"That she did. How well did you know her?"

"Not a bit." His grin was practically serene.

The fat man lifted one heavy hand without moving his elbow from the table and Nate looked at him.

"This fella a cop?" asked the fat man.

"Him?" Nate laughed. "He's an ex-con, for God's sake."

"So why're you answering his questions?"

"I don't know." Nate looked at me. "Why do I answer your questions?"

"You're just natural-born polite."

"Well," said the fat man, smiling, "we come here to eat—you mind?"

Of course I didn't so Rose took their orders and when she left the fat man sipped from his water glass and gazed at me.

"You must be Carl Wilcox—the fella that beat Nate here when he was just a kid."

"Uh-huh. That was right after he'd about cold-crocked me without bothering to come around in front."

The fat man's dark eyebrows lifted as he turned to Nate. "I didn't hear about that part."

Nate laughed easy. "When a boy tackles Wilcox, he takes any advantage handy."

The fat man grinned and shook his head. "You, Nate, you are a rascal."

Nate agreed with that and they both chuckled and enjoyed it all so much it made me tired.

Before I could push any more, Orrie walked in, blinked in the dim light, spotted Nate and waddled over to take a chair at the table and sit down with a sigh. He knew the fat man—called him Jack Wortle in a respectful tone—and asked him how Nate was doing. Just fine, said the fat man.

"I don't want to bother you none," said Orrie, "but I got to ask Nate a couple questions. It's just routine."

"How come?"

"Well," said Orrie, shifting uncomfortably, "this here killing we've had—it's a real unusual case—so I got to check out everything different that happened during the weekend. Now Nate's been gone about six months. I know he hasn't written to his ma or been in touch with anybody in Corden all that time. So last Saturday he shows up for a visit so I got to get the whole story, see?"

"Orrie," said Nate grandly, "you ask me anything you like."

"Okay," said Orrie, obviously relieved that Nate was in

54

a generous mood. "Now Flory was in your graduating class and you must've known her some—you ever offer to take her home?"

"Could be, Orrie—I guess I tried every girl in Corden, one time or another."

"When was the last time you asked?"

"Probably the last time I saw her."

"When was that?"

"Oh, quite a while ago."

Orrie looked at him a little harder, leaned forward and rested his elbows on the table. "She ever let you?"

Nate tried to look sorrowful. "You're gonna ruin my reputation, Orrie."

"What's that mean?"

"Well, you know, folks around Corden, they figure Nate's very handy with the girls—but if you want to know the truth, Flory never gave me a tumble. Not one."

"I see." Orrie looked down at the table for a second, then raised his eyes. "You remember asking her for a dance last Saturday night?"

"Sounds familiar. I was a little smashed—you know?"

"And she turned you down flat."

"If you say so."

"And you got nasty."

"So what'd you expect—I'd kiss her ass?"

He still looked friendly but his voice was hard.

"You waited for her outside, after the dance, didn't you?"

"Yeah, I did. I was gonna apologize. I felt bad, you know? And then the Goddamned Lard-ass saw me when he came out ahead of her and damned near broke my head against the wall—"

The fat man shifted his gaze from Orrie to Nate and the smile was gone from his round face. Orrie caught the change and his voice took an edge.

"What'd you do after that?"

"I went up to Lil's. Got laid and went back to Loden."

"What time'd you leave Lil's?"

"Hell, I don't know—who watches the clock up there?"

"And then you drove straight west, huh?"

"Like an arrow," he said cheerfully.

Orrie shook his head and gazed around the café.

"Ain't this something? Nobody's got an alibi worth a fart. A whole mob could've done that girl in, what with all the guys who could've been out back. If I find a man with a real alibi I'm bound to figure he done it—everybody else is too damned dumb."

He stood, hitched up his pants and scowled murder.

"Okay," he told Nate, "just don't go making any sudden trips anyplace distant without letting me know—you got that?"

"Don't worry, I ain't going anyplace—you just keep your eye on old Carl here—he's the traveling man."

I smiled at him and marveled at the mellowness I'd taken on in my advanced years. Of course my tolerance was helped some by the fact I'd already knocked his block off once.

Orrie drifted out into the sunlight and I tagged along.

"Did Doc finish his autopsy on Flory?" I asked.

"Uh-huh."

"What'd he find?"

He glanced at me and squinted against the sun. "She died from getting beat on the head with a iron pipe, probably an inch and a half—rusty."

"Yeah, I know she was knocked down, but was she knocked up?"

He stopped so sudden I took a step beyond and had to turn to face him.

"Now where in the hell did you get that notion?"

56

"Hell, Orrie, it's a thing that happens to girls now and then—and it could be why she got killed."

Orrie snorted and waddled on. "All right, she was knocked up. And I figure whoever poked it into her knocked her dead—she met him there to talk about it— either trying to lever some money out of him, or get him to marry her. It's the big reason I got to figure it wasn't you— you weren't around when she was having fun—and if you had been—she'd sure as hell not expect you to come up with any money, let alone a ring. She was something like five months along—maybe even more according to Doc— and nobody's noticed a thing except she quit seeing guys and wasn't talking much. I figure it must've been a tough time for that little girl, huh?"

We arrived in front of City Hall and stood there a moment, squinting against the sun and feeling the heat reflected from the brick wall. A little whirlwind formed in the street and swept a wild cone of dust across the walk to our right. Orrie watched it die, then peered at me.

"You notice Gus didn't show up at the restaurant? How many times you been in his place when he didn't show?"

"Damned few."

"Damned right—he's been a hermit since Flory got killed—but I tell you—I just can't see him killing anybody—not that way."

"Yeah, it was more like something Nate'd do," I said.

He nodded. "I thought of that."

"Was she raped?"

"Doc says she wasn't sexually molested. I think that means she wasn't."

"If that's right, I'd be surprised if it was Nate."

"Maybe he was too drunk to get it up."

"Then he'd probably have fallen asleep before he could club anybody."

Orrie grunted, suggested we get out of the damned sun

and led the way inside where the big room that housed the fire rig and jail cell managed to cool the air that blew through the open doors and out the back windows. By night, I remembered, the breeze usually died and left the place hotter than a bakery oven.

Orrie plunked his broad butt on the desk chair, glanced down and suddenly leaned forward.

"Well, looky here—"

"What?"

"A note." He read it and raised his eyebrows. "How about that?"

"Cut the cackle—what's it say?"

He grinned and handed it over to me.

"To Orrie—" it began. *"You are too dum to live—why ain't Carl Wilcox in jail? Search his room. That hotel. His truck. Get off your big fat ass and do something about Flory's awful murder."*

It had been printed in pencil on a pulp tablet with childish block letters.

"Pretty cute," I said, handing it back to Orrie.

"You mean mentioning the truck last? Yeah—or maybe he just wanted to make me sweat awhile so I'd be good and ripe when I found the pipe. Well, we're gonna have to make this look good. I'll call Deputy Torkelson to help and that'll make it nice and public."

Deputy Torkelson was tall and bony with a double-hinged jaw that wouldn't allow him more than thirty seconds of silence at a stretch. He showed up about ten minutes after Orrie's call and by the time we got to the back lot half a dozen citizens had drifted on to the scene. Orrie went through the truck cab, the motor and over the back, including the underside, while Torkelson mostly hovered around, looking bug-eyed and offering suggestions when he wasn't asking questions.

"It'd be a billy club or maybe some kinda pipe, wouldn't

it? A thing like that, a fella could hide most anywheres, eh?"

"Uh-huh," said Orrie as he backed out from under the truck and dusted off his pants. He was putting on such a great act I kept wondering if he'd forgotten we'd already found the weapon.

"What'll we search next?" asked Torkelson eagerly.

"I'll tell you what—you go through that trash barrel over there, then check the fence by Christenson's garage and then go through the Wilcox garage and the Dodge parked in there. And keep this mob back—I don't want them messing things up. Come on, Carl, we'll go up to your room and go through that."

Bertha watched balefully as we passed through her kitchen and Orrie eyed the doughnut jar but didn't dast help himself and she didn't offer.

He was owly as we went up the servants' narrow stairway.

"That woman'd oughtta lose a hundred pounds—everything she wears fits like a saddle on a sow."

"You just figure no woman's got a right to outweigh you—what the hell, Orrie—who cares how the duds fit if the chow's good?"

I should've kept my mouth shut. I'd figured we'd sit on my bed and shoot the breeze awhile but Orrie was actually bastard enough to take advantage and search my room. First off he found the bottle of booze and took a swig—to test it, he said.

"Not bad—is this Boswell's moonshine?"

"As a matter of fact," I said, "it's a urine sample I was planning to show Doc."

"Wouldn't surprise me none," he said, shoving the cork back, "you probably drink enough to piss ninety proof—but how'd you get it so clear?"

"Clean living."

He grunted and put the bottle back in the drawer. He pawed through my underwear, socks, flannel shirts and pretty soon pulled out the *Rubáiyát* and a copy of Moore's poems. After a high-browed glance at me, he opened the Moore and read the inscription. It was to me from Ma for my birthday, 1926. The cover was red leather with gold trim.

Orrie thumbed through a few pages, as if expecting to find something hidden between leaves and finally put it back on the bureau.

"You read this stuff?"

"Naw—I just press flowers in it."

"Huh." He gave up on the bureau and waddled around to the foot of my bed where I kept my trunk. "What's in this?"

"Bodies. I keep 'em all in there."

"Uh-huh. Open her up, let's take a look."

"You already know where the Goddamned pipe is."

"Sure I do—but I don't often get a chance to check a man out like this and I wouldn't be smart to pass it up now, would I?"

"You're a nosy Goddamned fart," I told him, but I opened the trunk and then sat down on the bed.

He examined buffalo horns, natural and polished, arrow- and spearheads, a tomahawk with a cracked handle, beaded leather pouches, moccasins, spurs and a lariat along with picture postcards and photos. Orrie went through every card and picture, hoping, I guessed, to find some hot French stuff. At first he squatted on his heels, then, as the stuff piled up around him, he sat down on his wide butt. When he'd gone through the last card and found nothing racier than a picture of a naked baby, he sighed and glared up at me.

"You were right—there's nothing in here but dead bodies."

"I hardly ever lie."

He got up, grunting with the effort, and stood a moment in the middle of the mess, looking almost thoughtful.

"How come there ain't any guns or knives in this junk?"

"I'm a peaceful fella—what'd I want tools for mayhem for?"

"Didn't you ever pack a gun?"

"Once."

"How come you had a gun that time?"

"How else you gonna hold up a jewelry store?"

He shook his head. "Carl, you gotta be the God-damnedest madman I ever met. Why'd you want to rob a jewelry store?"

"It was quicker than trying to borrow money from a bank."

"Come on, what really happened?"

"Well, I'd got friendly with a widow woman who needed money—I won't tell you the whole story—it chokes me up so I can't talk—anyway I went to this jewelry store which was handy, showed the jeweler my gun and asked for a loan. All that tightwad wanted to talk about was when would I pay it back and while we were working on that an old couple walked in. I showed them the gun and asked them to lay down behind the counter but the old lady had on a white dress and just flat out refused—she wasn't going to get that outfit all dusty if it meant dying but she offered to hold her hands up and did. Her husband—I guess it was her husband—claimed he had a bad shoulder and wondered if it was all right if he just held his hands folded behind his back? About then this dumb cop wandered by, saw the lady with her hands up and charged in like the Lone Ranger, waving his cannon. His caliber was twice mine and I figured he had shells in it and I knew I didn't so I put my piece on the counter and told the jeweler to forget about the loan. Later, when the judge stopped laughing, he gave me a year and said he hoped I'd learned something."

"So you learned never to pack an empty gun?"

"No, I learned never to let an old lady stand in the middle of a jewelry store in front of a window with her hands up."

That left Orrie speechless and he got up and started out the door.

"You forgot to look under the bed," I told him.

"By God, I did." And he actually got down on his fat knees and rubbernecked around. "Clean. Your ma must make the maid do your room—does she come up with her to make sure you don't get in the maid's pants?"

"Orrie, Ma knows if I want in the maid I'll manage—now do you plan to put my stuff back in the trunk?"

"I'd never get it straight," he said. "So long."

So I repacked the trunk with its lifetime accumulation of a saddle tramp and then went over to Boswell's hoping we could share a snort and some talk but he was out. For a while I sat in his cluttered shack, staring at boxes of junk he'd gathered and that didn't cheer me any. I decided the only thing more miserable than a bachelor was an old bachelor. Or maybe an old married man.

CHAPTER
9

Around four-thirty I drifted down to Gus's Café and found Joel sitting at a rear table with Rose, drinking coffee. When I joined them she got up to bring me a cup and they sat side by side, watching in silence while I built a cigarette and lit up.

"Where's Gus?" I asked.

"He was in for a while," said Rose, "but he was feeling poorly and went home. We think he's sick."

"He sure looks lousy," said Joel.

"You figure he was sweet on Flory?" I asked.

"Sure—who wasn't?" said Joel.

"I wish I knew." I stared at him and he looked back. His straw hair flopped over his acned forehead, and the big nose jutting from between his narrow eyes was so wide I doubt he could see a moth perched on its tip. He was one of those rare homely guys who could stand close examination and hand back a grin that said if you didn't like what you saw, you could go screw yourself.

"How long you been working for Gus—four years?"

"More like five."

"I guess you get along okay, huh?"

"Like soul mates. He makes money. I make meals. It works out fine for him so he treats me okay."

"He told me he was too strict with Flory. He figures that's why she decided to quit."

Joel added a few grains of sugar to his coffee, stirred it and took a sip.

"Did you think he was too strict with her?" I asked.

"If that's what he said, that's what he believes. Gus don't lie."

"Uh-huh. But we all see things a little different. Now Lard says Flory did as she pleased around here—even left early now and again. That doesn't sound like tough to me."

Joel shrugged. "Maybe that just means that Gus wasn't around all the time."

"Lard says you helped clean up for her when she left early."

He gave me a puckish grin. "So I'm neat—what's that prove?"

"Damned if I know. I'd just like to figure out why Flory quit here and what made her change from a butterfly to an ant. There's gotta be a damned good reason for that."

"Maybe she just got sick of the hassle—all the guys hanging around and deals like Lard strong-arming the competition."

"Did she ever say she was sick of the guys?"

"Not that I heard."

"Well," said Rose, "she never said it out like that, but she told me once they were all a bunch of stupid kids. That was right after Lard threatened Will."

We sat silently for a few seconds before I asked if Nate had been in on Saturday night.

Joel shrugged and Rose frowned thoughtfully.

"Seems like he was—we were awful busy—sometimes I get the nights mixed up—you know?"

God, did I know.

"Who was helping wait tables?" I asked.

"Oh, Dedee was here—and Mrs. Gardner."

"Claire?"

"Uh-huh. She comes in busy times—keeps things organized. She's been running things, you know. She's big on that."

She always had been. Claire was Judge Simon's only daughter and she wanted her daddy to be governor from the time she was about eight years old and visited the capital with him when he was a legislator. She couldn't begin the promotion until she was seventeen but by the time she was twenty she'd shifted into high gear. Jake Driscoll, a ward heeler from the west hill, told me it was enough to make a man cry to see that girl's brains and energy wasted on promoting her stuffed-shirt old man.

"If she'd run on her own, she'd have won hands down," he told me. He tried to make it sound like he was kidding but I could tell he meant it. She had looks and savvy and even better, she had class.

Her pa lost by a hair and she never quite recovered. I suppose it was the first time in her life she'd missed what she went after. She did manage to wangle a seat on the federal bench for papa before she announced she was through with politics.

Elihu told me he figured she married Gus because she spotted him as a future political candidate.

"He was a gawky, old-shoe type fella that people trusted and listened to because he was a lot more than half smart. The trouble was, I figure, he was too smart—he couldn't stand making enemies and he knew damned well the minute you pick a party and run for office, you already got half the world hating you. He couldn't manage that. Hell, he couldn't take sides in a boxing match if he was one of the fighters."

What had interested me most about Claire stories was her promotion style. Rumors kept floating around that when she was politicking for pa she messed around with men who had political muscle and could back her games. Nasty types called her the Battery Girl—Eveready Claire.

Most claimed she got by with parties, smiles and eye promises.

I always figured she married Gus on the rebound from her love affair with politics. He was younger than Claire by three years or so. They moved to Sioux Falls where he was something of a hotshot in real estate until the Depression made him lose his shirt and suddenly he was back in Corden running the café which must have been bank-rolled by the judge. Claire disappeared behind the stone wall and tall pines that hid their white house on the west hill which had been left to Gus by his grandma.

"I don't remember seeing Claire around here," I said to Rose.

"You haven't been around lately on a busy night—we don't serve anything strong enough for you. But she's been coming in—what, Joel—about a year now?"

"Since after New Year's."

"How does Gus feel about that?" I asked.

"I don't think he was exactly tickled pink—but you know Gus—he never said anything."

"How'd Flory react?"

"Flory?" Rose frowned. "Why'd she care—it didn't mean anything to her."

"It must've meant another boss. Did she ever leave early when Claire was around?"

"She never left early on any busy night. Flory wouldn't let us down like that."

"How'd she get along with the boss lady?"

"Just fine. Mrs. Gardner liked her, just the way every-body else did—isn't that right, Joel?"

"Yeah." Joel nodded.

"But Flory wasn't around long after Claire started com-ing in, was she?" I asked.

"Well, no—I guess it was only two or three weeks."

"What'd Claire do when the big blowup came—I mean when Gus yelled at Flory?"

"She didn't say a word—she just watched," said Rose.

"How'd you know that?" asked Joel. "You were too busy gawking at Gus to notice."

"Well, maybe—I know she didn't *say* anything."

"What'd you notice?" I asked him.

"When Gus first started, I heard him and came out because I thought he must be mad at a customer and maybe there was bad trouble. Then I saw it was Flory he was jawing and I looked at Mrs. Gardner who was right by the kitchen door and she had a real little smile—just for a second. Then she saw me and frowned and jerked her head for me to get back in my hole."

"You figure it was a happy smile or a funny smile?"

"I ain't that expert on smiles," he said, and got up to start things for supper.

I went out to the hot street and drifted back to the hotel. It was obvious I was going to have to get acquainted with Claire Gardner but it was going to be a bother because she didn't ever visit the pool hall or the hotel and I wasn't exactly a regular at the Congregational Church. It'd have to be in her territory.

CHAPTER
10

A little after supper on Saturday night I drifted into Gus's place and found Claire, directing the help, clearing off tables and guiding people to places. She was casual about it—you could hardly hear her voice if she wasn't talking to you—yet she was in total command. I sat down at the counter, ordered cherry pie and coffee and went to work on them while watching her, mostly through the mirror beyond the counter. I figured she must be forty but she looked ten years younger—slim, smooth-faced, a little shiny like an expensive new doll. I kept watching, letting her know it, and decided she was a mite too tight in the ass—I like a fanny with more round—and way too stiff-necked for me. But she had a classy carriage and there's something about a snooty woman that gets to me. I like the challenge of trying to work through all of the antagonism—and if I can't make it I still get a kick out of trying. It doesn't tear me all up to strike out.

I must've been watching her for nearly fifteen minutes before she slowed down enough in passing for me to speak.

"Ever take a break?" I asked.

She lifted a thin brow and said, "I don't come here to rest."

Ten more minutes passed while I nursed a cup of coffee and chinned with Tad Skinner, who clerked at the local hardware. Tad wasn't inspirational but he was one guy who never treated me different after I came back from stir and didn't ask stupid questions. He liked to sit in the café Saturday nights and watch the girls.

"What do you think of Claire?" I asked him.

"You mean Mrs. Gardner?"

"Yeah."

"Oh, she's a real lady, that one."

"You think she's sexy?"

Tad was too young to think a woman over thirty ever thought of sex and he was shocked. He told me again that she was a lady.

"What makes her a lady—that tight-style ass?"

He shook his head. "You shouldn't talk like that, Carl."

"Who'd you think it was all right to talk about—Rose? You figure she's sexy?"

He nearly pulled an eye muscle trying to look around without moving his head. "Uh, yeah, sure."

"She's just a kid. Now your real sexy woman is one with experience—like Claire."

"Carl, she can see you're talking about her—she won't like it."

"Everybody used to talk about her—ever hear about how she worked to make her daddy governor?"

"No—he's been a judge as long as I can remember."

"You should've been around sooner—you missed a lot."

"Well, nobody's been around that showed up for the beginning."

I was still watching Claire but that crack made me grin and for her that was too much. She came over and leaned against the counter end. I was sitting at the last stool near the kitchen.

"Why do you sit there, gawking and grinning at me?"

"Glad you asked—first, because you're good to look at, and second because I want to talk to you. Tad, you mind moving for a bit—we'd like a little privacy."

He gave me a horrified look and slipped off the stool. I got up, offered my place to Claire and sat down where Tad had been.

Claire perched and frowned at me.

"When you plan to redecorate this place?" I asked.

"Don't tell me you're looking for a job?"

"I could handle it," I said, looking around, "and as is, the joint just isn't high-toned enough for a woman with your style."

"I can't see that is any of your concern—what do you really want from me?"

"I'd like to learn a little about Flory—what do you figure she wanted?"

"I'm sure I don't know." Her eyes left me for a moment as she watched Dedee clearing a table nearby.

"How much notice did she give?" I asked.

She rolled her hazel eyes at me. The whites were so clear I expected to hear a click when they stopped.

"None."

"She wasn't maybe fired, was she?"

"Isn't that academic now?"

"I don't think so. For some reason that girl changed from a flirty kid to a loner between the time she worked here and went to the hotel. What happened?"

"All I know is, she quit, and now, if you'll excuse me, I have things to do."

I watched her tight rear as she walked to the kitchen, lifted my coffee cup to find it empty and started to leave just as Gus came out of the kitchen. His face had aged ten years since I'd seen him last and he walked as if the movement hurt him. When I said hi he pretended to be surprised and stopped.

"You on the wagon, Carl?" he asked, looking at my cup.

"Temporarily. Strained my elbow Saturday night—giving it a little rest."

He gave me a thin smile. "Well, how do things look, considering?"

"Not as clear as I'd expect. You told me Flory quit—you real sure she wasn't fired?"

He looked pained. "That's a thing I'd know for sure, Carl—and why'd I lie to you?"

"I don't know. How'd Flory and Claire get along?"

"Just fine, why wouldn't they?"

"From what I hear—it wasn't much more than a week after Claire started helping out when Flory left."

"It was three weeks."

"My error. Three weeks. And she gave no notice."

"That's right. I told you—I hurt her feelings and she quit."

"How'd Claire feel about that?"

"About what—Flory quitting—?"

"About you bawling out the help in front of the public."

He looked a little sheepish and a great deal miserable.

"She said I should have done it in the kitchen, where nobody'd hear. Of course she was right."

"Who was at the table when you lit into her?"

He looked blank for a second and then said, "I don't know—no idea—"

"Come on, Gus, you know everybody's name and most people's history—you had a whole tableful of fellows and you can't remember a one?"

"It was a busy night, Carl—I was upset. I admit it—I just didn't pay any attention to anything but that Flory was wasting too much time—she'd done it before—"

"With the same bunch?"

"I told you—I don't remember who they were—excuse me—"

If I'd been a cop I'd have taken him to City Hall and sweated him some but that wasn't possible so I took a stroll down by the Playhouse and looked in. It was still too early for the action. By ten Louie Little's musical pirates would be playing arrangements stolen from famous bands with a drummer who had all the imagination of a metronome and six amateurs trying to sound like forty professionals. It wouldn't matter—the crowd didn't hear much but the beat and a good share of them couldn't follow that.

Orrie was gabbing with Paul Lindstrom, the Playhouse owner, and a moment after noticing me he waddled over to my side, swabbing his face with a wrinkled blue bandanna.

"It's a damned shame we can't store up some of this heat for January," he said. "You been learning anything?"

"Maybe—let's take a hike."

We headed west up the hill.

"It sounds like this to me," I began. "Claire came to the café because she got suspicious something was going on between Flory and Gus. And pretty soon she sees Gus blow his top because Flory is flirting with a bunch of young guys. That same night Flory quits. Gus tells me they were so busy he didn't even know who the guys were and admits that Claire gave him a hard time because he bawled Flory out in public. But I think she quit because she was mad at being bawled out in front of Claire—you know—there's nothing in the world so bad as being put down in front of your lover—except having your lover put you down in front of the competition."

We were a block away from the Playhouse by then but Orrie looked around nervously.

I stopped to roll a cigarette and he unwrapped a cigar. After we shared his match we stood puffing and watching bugs circle the streetlight overhead.

"Awright," said Orrie, "Gus was fooling around with Flory, Claire got wise—moved into the café and broke up the game. So, now what've you got? Flory leaves and everything's taken care of. Why'd anybody kill Flory because of any of that?"

"Because she was pregnant and tried to lean on somebody for money."

He thought about that and shook his head. "It don't make sense to me."

"Well, the trouble is, murder doesn't have to make sense. Most of the time I bet it doesn't."

"If it don't make sense, what good's figuring it all out?"

"Because it makes some sense. I figure you have to think about it in a way you and I wouldn't be concerned with ordinarily."

"You mean it's like the old Indian said, 'If everybody thought alike they'd all want my squaw'?"

"Exactly. I mean, can't you just imagine how a woman like Claire'd feel about some whippersnapper kid taking away a man she didn't figure was good enough for her to begin with?"

"You trying to tell me Claire hit Flory?"

"She'd probably liked to have—but no—I can't picture her doing it. No—I figure she'd arrange things."

"That'd be her style," he admitted. "But who'd she pick around here?"

"Well, lots of young fellas come to town on Saturdays, and most of them wind up at Gus's Café. You know everybody in town six days a week—but Saturday night a quarter of the crowd's strangers."

"I know most of 'em—except the young ones—"

"So that's probably where she'd recruit."

"You truly got yourself convinced, huh? How the hell you figure we're gonna prove a thing like that?"

"Orrie—you can't solve a murder by figuring out the handiest way to prove who did it—first you got to decide who did it—all the proving comes later."

He gave me a disgusted look, chewed his cigar and muttered something about smartasses.

"Lemme know when you got it all doped out," he said at last, and headed back toward the dance hall.

I thought some of going to visit Boswell for a drink or twelve but couldn't fit into the mood and wound up in my room at the hotel where I had a belt from the bureau jug and then stretched out and smoked while I thought things over. I was getting nowhere fast when heavy steps approached down the hall and there was a sharp rap on my door.

"Yeah?"

Orrie pushed in, sat down on the straight-backed chair and handed me a piece of ruled paper.

"You dumbass," it read, *"if you hadn't been so slow you'd have the murder weapon alredy. Now you got to serch the damned dump for it. That's where Wilcox hid it."*

CHAPTER
11

It was so hot by noon that even the grasshoppers were hugging shade. Orrie had a crew of four men sifting through garbage and trash along the west slope of the dump while he kept to the firm ground where he could admire the view as much as he was able through his sweat and squint.

"According to my old man," he told me, "all you got to do to find a thing that's lost is say, 'If I was a whatchama-callit, where'd I be?' And then you go there and you'll find it. Only I already know where this Goddamned whatcha-macallit is but I got to pertend otherwise because of your dumb idea."

"It's pure hell," I agreed.

"You and Doc figured we'd spot the tipper-offer—but he ain't stuck around long enough to be spotted."

"Yeah, I noticed."

The search had been going on for a little over half an hour when Deputy Torkelson came up with a length of pipe about half a rod from where I'd dumped my trash load. He picked it from beside an old icebox with his gloved hand and carried it gingerly, like a stick of dyna-mite, to Orrie. He didn't mind grinning at me a bit.

"How about this, Orrie? You figure it's the piece?"

"Sure looks right," said Orrie. He turned to me. "This familiar to you?"

"See one hunk of pipe, you've seen 'em all."

"Looks like there's blood on it," said Torkelson happily. He was so proud it made his chest stretch like a bullfrog's throat at croaking time.

"More likely rust," I said.

All the dump crew gathered around. They stared at the pipe and a couple snuck peeks at me. Orrie told Torkelson to hold the pipe up closer and looked it over carefully. It was shorter than the piece we'd taken from my truck but was the same otherwise. It looked bloodstained all right.

Orrie squinted at me. Sweat stood on his forehead and nose and trickled down from his temple. "You remember throwing anything like this off your truck, Carl?"

"Everything I threw off the truck is in that pile where you started. I didn't hike in the dump or throw anything. I didn't see this piece and I'll bet some son of a bitch who can't spell planted it there last night."

Orrie had Torkelson take him back to where he'd found the pipe and after some time he came back and suggested we all go back to town.

"You gonna lock him up?" asked Torkelson.

"You figure I should, Deputy?"

"Well yeah, I'd say so if you was to ask me."

"I asked, didn't I?"

Torkelson nodded and grinned a little broader. "You want I should put the cuffs on him?"

"No," said Orrie, "and you needn't start building a gallows just yet either. Come on, let's go."

I rode with Orrie in his Model T and Torkelson followed with the crew in his Chevy.

"I'm gonna have to lock you up for a while," said Orrie. "If I don't, the whole town'll be on my ass."

"That's damned foolishness—we already did what we were trying to do—we proved somebody's trying to frame me."

"Naw—not to this town we ain't. I ain't dumb enough to believe you're pulling all this rigamarole for a lark— you're crazy enough for almost anything but you been sober a good many days and you wouldn't go setting up a lynch mob after yourself just to keep from getting bored—"

"So what the hell you think your killer's gonna do now—lead a lynch mob?"

"He might."

"Like hell—he can leave it up to somebody else— Torkelson maybe—listen—does Torkelson hang around Gus's place? He ever talk to Claire?"

"I suppose so—he's been there—hell—everybody has."

So I settled down in the cell behind the fire engine and Orrie brought me a couple books from the city library which was also the town hall meeting room just behind his office.

The books were *Tarzan and the Jewels of Opar* and *Tarzan the Terrible.*

"How come you picked these?" I asked.

"I couldn't find any Shakespeare. If you want *Pilgrim's Progress*, I know where that is."

"You sure you don't want me to sign these out?"

"Naw, you're not going anywhere."

Before I got around to any reading, Hank showed up and I asked him if the natives were getting restless. He said there hadn't been a soul stirring on Main Street all afternoon but if folks realized how cool the jail was I'd have lots of company. The windows were open and bars don't slow down a breeze worth mentioning.

"Are there bugs in there?" asked Hank, staring at the bunk suspiciously.

"Only me—the bunk's too hard for bugs."

"Has Orrie charged you with murder?"

"He wants me to think I'm in protective custody. I don't know what he's let on to the mob."

"Shouldn't you have a lawyer?"

"From this town?"

"Maybe Grandpa could get one from the Cities."

"Yeah, and maybe I'll piss purple come next coronation day. Listen—how about you go ask Boswell to make a visit?"

"Sure—right now?"

"No, be a little more casual. Just drop him the word I'd like to see him a little after dusk."

He said okay and after shooting the breeze a bit more, went off.

At supper time Torkelson brought me a meal from Gus's place and I ate while trying to figure why food carried two blocks in desert heat turned cold before a man could get it to his mouth. Torkelson parked out in the front office most of the time but once in a while strolled in to grin at me. I began to feel like a hog being fattened for market.

It was just past early dusk when I heard movement outside my window. This window, I forgot to mention, was a good six feet off the floor. Torkelson had looked in a few minutes before so I didn't figure he was due back for half an hour. I stood against the wall and watched sharp. After a few seconds something came through the opening over-head. I couldn't make out what the hell at first but then I saw it was a pint bottle tied to a pole with twine.

"Boswell," I told myself. "The old fart's delivering on schedule."

The pole tip brushed the cell window top and lowered smoothly until the bottle dangled a foot above my head. I reached up, untied the knot, tugged the twine and immediately the pole was withdrawn. I managed to laugh without a sound but before I could move to my bunk, Deputy Torkelson said, "I'll take that, Wilcox."

He actually had a gun in his paw, pointed at my nose. "Just hand it over," he said.

I could feel the mad coming up in a rush and moved toward him. He stepped back, holding the gun steady.

"Just shove it through the bars at the bottom, set it on the floor and move back."

"It ain't nitro," I said. "I'm not gonna bust out."

"Booze ain't legal," he told me with a straight face. "You set it there where I told you or I'll part your head right in the middle."

He was all full of excitement from the unfamiliar power he felt in the gun and the bars that protected him. I considered dropping the bottle out of sheer spite but in his state, and being so fond of me, I could imagine him opening fire and later claiming he'd shot in self-defense when I attacked him with the bottle even though it was only a pint.

I put the bottle on the floor, shoved it through the bars, went back to my bunk and sat down. Torkelson casually shoved his gun in its holster, picked up the bottle, uncorked it and took a slug. It went down hard. He wiped his mouth with the back of his hand and shook his head.

"Jesus—old Boswell must've made that this afternoon."

"If it's too raw I'll gladly take it off your hands."

"I bet you would." He took another slug. "I dunno— maybe I'd ought to let you have it after all—might save the cost of hanging."

I agreed but he only grinned and went back to the office.

Half an hour later I heard scraping outside the cell window and guessed that Boswell had overheard what happened and was returning with reinforcements. I went to the cell door, looked toward the front and listened. There wasn't a sound. I turned and there, in the window beyond the bars, was Boswell's shaggy head. It gave me a hell of a shock—I just couldn't picture the old bastard on a ladder but he had to be unless he'd sprouted wings that evening.

"What's this?" I whispered. "Hourly deliveries?"

He said "Shh!" and stuck his arm through the window. In his fist was a quart bottle. I reached up and took it.

"How come you only brought a pint the first time?" I asked.

"Didn't."

I thought that over a second. "Listen—Boswell, go around and talk to Torkelson. Tell him you want to visit me."

"He won't let me."

"Ask him."

"Already did. Nearly an hour ago. He said no."

"So try again—he can't any more than say no again."

He sighed, pulled back and a moment later I heard a scraping as he removed the ladder. It wasn't long after before he came scuttling across the concrete floor past the fire engine.

"Okay," he said, "what'd you want?"

"Isn't Torkelson out there?"

"Yup—asleep. Got a pint beside him—spilled—"

"You sure he's asleep?"

"Head's down, eyes closed—didn't answer—"

"Did you bring a bottle earlier?"

"No—I was gonna come and tell you I'd hand one in later but Torky wouldn't let me—"

"Somebody shoved a bottle through the window— Torkelson took it from me and tried it. Go get Orrie—hurry up!"

Boswell gave me a horrified look and hurried off. I opened the jug he'd left and sniffed at the mouth thoughtfully. It didn't have quite the bouquet of roses but I figured if I didn't hit it then I might lose my nerve. Besides, anybody cute enough to have all of Boswell's store poisoned was going to get me sooner or later, so why wait?

I'd put only a modest dent in the supply when I heard Orrie arrive and things got excited in the front room. I corked the quart, stuck it under the hard pillow on the cot and waited.

In a few seconds Orrie waddled in followed by two of his dump-grounds crew.

"Tell me what happened," said Orrie, "everything."

It didn't take long.

"Son of a bitch," he muttered. "All you saw was the pole and twine—didn't this guy say anything?"

"Nary a word."

"Son of a bitch!"

"Is Torkelson done?"

"Sure as hell." His eyes were moist.

"Well, that's too bad. You gonna let me out now?"

He scowled, stuck his chin out and demanded, "Why should I?"

"Well, damn it, I sure as hell didn't poison Torkelson—somebody was after me and he took it—that's open enough for even you to see—"

"All I know is you was here alone with Torky, and now he's dead. Maybe you managed it all—maybe you had it on you when we brought you in—I didn't search you."

It was plain he was bad upset and while it about choked me to do it, I kept my voice calm.

"Okay, so why'd I kill him?"

"You figured he was after your hide—you said as much this afternoon."

"Orrie, for Christ's sake—I haven't been out of your sight except when I was in here since Torkelson started getting snotty with me—you think I had him pegged early enough to set this up—or do you figure I always carry a bottle of poisoned booze in case I meet a bastard?"

He waved his arm wearily and looked away. "I'm damned if I know what to figure—but you're gonna stay right here for the night—and that's flat."

He swung around and hiked out with his stooges trailing behind.

I took the quart from under the pillow and after enough belts from that could have slept on a skewer and the cot was good as a featherbed.

Orrie turned me loose just before noon the next day. Doc had tested the stains on the pipe we'd found in the public search and they weren't from human blood. Orrie was owly enough by then to suggest that made it mine but he didn't offer to take a sample. There was about half of Boswell's moonshine left and since it was too big to smuggle out I offered it to Orrie. He made gagging sounds and told me to shove it up my rear. I couldn't believe he'd been all that fond of Torkelson and decided it was the principle of the thing that got him—somebody knocking off his deputy right in City Hall. The fact it was an accident didn't ease anything for Orrie. I think he wanted to blame me for not gulping the pint instead of handing it over when Torky asked.

I stopped by the kitchen in the hotel, hoping I'd find Bertha in a good mood and bum a decent breakfast but Ma was there and all I got was a hard time.

"Another man dead," said Ma, "thanks to your weakness for liquor."

I asked her pardon for living and took off for Gus's Café.

Rose was serving a couple truck drivers when I walked in and Claire was in the back booth with Joel, planning the next day's menu. I slipped on to a stool toward the back and asked Rose if she'd fix me a breakfast I could eat. All Orrie'd brought me at the jail was cold toast and coffee.

Pretty soon I was into scrambled eggs and bacon while Rose leaned on the counter, watching.

"It seems like Orrie's having an awful time trying to tag you for the killings," she said.

"You can give him an A for trying."

She leaned closer. "You got any idea who tried to give you poison?"

"I don't know who—or why—but thinking about it doesn't help my appetite."

She apologized and I apologized back for complaining when she'd treated me so fine and we were being sweet as hell when Claire got up from the booth and moseyed over. The light was strong in the café, reflecting hard off the white false front of the hardware store across the street. Claire moved so it was behind her and perched on the stool one removed from my right.

"The breakfast is on Gus," she said, "to make up for your hard times."

"That still go if I order pancakes now?"

Claire smiled and glanced at Rose who signaled Joel into action.

I drank coffee and tried to study Claire. The backlighting made her face vague and her hair unreal with light gleaming on the small loose ends.

"You must've decided I didn't do in Flory," I said.

"It begins to seem quite unlikely."

She smiled nice and easy and even though I had trouble seeing her because of the light in my eyes, I got a warm feeling in my gut that doesn't come from ordinary smiles. Hers was as intimate as an openmouthed kiss. I grinned back and more than likely looked a little sick. I glanced toward Rose who moved off to make busy work under the counter near the front windows. When I looked back at Claire I'd dumped the grin and almost managed to scowl.

"It's a curious thing," said Claire, before I could speak,

"but this is the first time I can remember when no one in Corden had anything to say about Carl's latest romantic involvement. Have you sworn off women?"

"No—I'm just having trouble finding an eligible widow."

"What happened to Jenny?"

"She met a traveling salesman. You know those fellas—very tough competition. Especially when I couldn't be around to guard the claim."

"That's too bad. She's a fine-looking woman—simple and sweet."

"No woman's just simple and sweet—but speaking of Jenny—was her boy Nate in here last night?"

"I don't believe I know him."

"Wiry fella—about twenty-two—curly haired, blue-eyed—lots of smile. He was one of the crowd interested in Flory."

"Is he tall?"

"Got about an inch on me."

"I may have seen him—I don't remember—but I'm not particularly observant of young people—they look so much alike. Why do you ask?"

"Oh, nothing special. I heard he was in town—he's been working west a ways until lately. I used to see a lot of Nate."

She smiled again. It came and went like a cloud formation—so smooth and gradual it was there and gone so quick you thought you imagined seeing it in the first place.

"I seem to remember hearing that you fought Nate once—that Jenny had you jailed for it. I'd guess that had more to do with your breakup than a traveling salesman."

"I'm flattered," I said, grinning at her. "I wouldn't have thought you'd kept track of a man like me."

"Oh, I know what goes on in Corden."

She glanced up as Rose delivered the plate of pancakes Joel had prepared and set them before me with a pitcher of syrup. A pat of butter was melting on the top cake and began a slow slide to my right.

"Bring Carl some more butter, Rose," said Claire.

I poured syrup and began working the fork.

"Until very lately," said Claire, "everyone in Corden knew almost all there was to know about everyone else. I imagine you know much about me—or think you do."

I eased off on the fork and took her in for a second. It was bothering me, looking into the light, and I thought of moving around her but instead looked in the counter mirror and took in her profile. It was damned good. Everything in perfect proportion, no sags or bulges. She might have been created on a drawing board. Her head turned until she met my eyes in the mirror. At the first meeting of our eyes I felt—not saw—something cold as a bare foot in the snow—and then the smile, like a tongue-touching kiss, was back.

"Lady," I said, "you got the most dangerous smile I ever saw. It ought to be illegal."

She laughed, letting me know she used it deliberately and at the same time admitting she was pleased. I turned away.

"Hey Rose—did you see Nate last night?"

She glanced at Claire, then at me. "Yes."

"When?"

"He ate supper—about five-thirty, I'd guess."

Claire left the stool and started toward the kitchen.

"Don't go away," I said.

"I assumed you were through questioning me."

"Now that makes it sound like you came around to be questioned—and I thought you were just being friendly."

Her smile became cold. "Why should I be friendly with you?"

"You know—that's just what throws me."

"Maybe it's your piratical charm," she said, and went back to the kitchen.

When Rose came over to fill my cup I asked if she'd ever noticed Claire talking with Nate. She said no, why'd I ask?

I ignored her question and asked if she was certain she'd never seen them talking.

She shook her head. "He's not the sort she talks to."

"Well, neither am I—that's what makes it all so interesting."

CHAPTER
12

At five-thirty I was in front of the courthouse waiting for Jenny. She looked startled at first, then smiled before she thought better of it and tried to turn casual.

"Well, out of jail again?"

"I hope it's not too big a disappointment."

"I'm glad you didn't get poisoned," she admitted. "I wouldn't want that to happen to anybody."

"You sure?"

"Fairly." She let the smile take over and I grinned back at her, wishing like hell she'd never had a kid named Nate and wasn't set on being a married lady. "How come you're here?"

"To walk you home."

"I already told you—I'm engaged."

"It won't ruin your life if I walk you home, will it?"

"Not likely," she said, and started walking.

"Being engaged must agree with you," I said, "you look just great."

She laughed easy and raised her head a little.

"You probably won't believe it when I tell you who said something good about you today."

She lifted her eyebrows. "Who?"

"Claire Gardner. She said you were a fine-looking woman."

Her pace slackened and she looked at me sharply.

"How did Claire Gardner happen to be talking about me?

"She was being sociable—wondered if we were still keeping company."

"As if she didn't know," she sniffed. Claire had that effect on most Corden women and I decided it had been dumb to mention her. "How is it she's so chummy all of a sudden with *you*?"

"Why, I guess she all of a sudden got on a democratic spell—that comes even to the high classes when they go in business and get worrying about customers. That's why your real aristocrats never take to trade—it makes people beholden to the common folk. Or maybe she was thinking about me almost being poisoned."

Jenny shook her head. "That must've been frightening—I mean—to know someone wanted to *kill* you—aren't you afraid?"

"What scares me most is I'm gonna be leery of taking free booze from now on, having to worry about whether I'll ever get to enjoy the hangover—"

"I would hope it'd make a sober man of you."

"It didn't scare me that much."

When we reached her front walk she stopped and turned to face me.

"Well, it was nice of you to walk me home—and I'm really glad you didn't get poisoned."

"I'm glad you're glad—but are you saying you don't want me to walk you up to your front door?"

"I haven't any beer—and there's nothing else I can offer you except coffee—and that's *all*."

"What more could a fellow ask?"

"There's no limit to what you'd ask for—or help yourself to. If I invite you in will you absolutely promise to behave?"

"Scout's honor."

"Danny's home, so don't embarrass me."

I wanted to ask about Nate but the Buick wasn't in sight and I was beginning to think he'd gone back to Loden. We walked up to the porch, climbed the two steps and I held the screen door for her. The hall was dark and cool. We stopped at the door to the living room and there was Danny on the wood and leather couch, reading a book. I greeted him and he called me Uncle Carl.

"He's not your uncle," said Jenny a little too sharply.

"I know," said Danny. He was about fourteen—a dark-haired, brown-eyed boy with a sober face and the dignity of an old Indian chief. He always seemed older than his brother Nate who had at least seven years on him. Sometimes he seemed older than Jenny.

"What're you reading?" I asked.

"*Archie and Mehitabel.*"

"Yeah? What's that about?"

"A cockroach and a cat. The cockroach types."

"Must have been a Southerner."

"That's where they grow big, huh?"

"Not generally as big as a cat."

He nodded and smiled vaguely before returning to the book.

I trailed Jenny who'd moved to the kitchen and was filling a coffeepot to heat on the kerosene stove. On the kitchen table, beside the north wall where windows looked out on the drive, I saw a cigarette-rolling machine.

"You taken to tobacco now?" I asked.

"No—Nate used it while he was here."

That shook me two ways—I was annoyed that the punk had taken over the cigarette machine which had practically been mine for four years—and it meant he was still around. That was what I'd expected when I'd walked her home, but for Jenny's sake I'd hoped I was wrong.

"He quit his job in Loden?"

"No—he just wanted to come home and see me."

"Uh-huh—and now he's gone back to work?"

She faced me squarely. "What is this—how come you're all of a sudden so interested in Nate?"

"I'm interested in anything that involves you, Jenny."

She shook her head slowly. "I can see one change prison made in you. In the old days you made remarks like that and I knew you were kidding and that you expected me to know it was just kidding. Now you try to sound convincing. They made a liar out of you, Carl."

"I can see some change in you too," I said. "You've turned from sharp to sour bitter."

"Maybe so—I got trained by an expert. So we don't like each other anymore—why're you here? What're you after?"

I was all at once mad, sick and sorry. The mad nearly took over but I choked it down and for several seconds didn't make a sound. Finally I got up and went toward the back door, passing just a few feet away from her as she stood by the stove.

"It's not that I don't like you anymore," I told her, "I'm never gonna forget how great we were—and nothing's gonna make me feel different about you. But I guess you're right in a way—we're different people now and it's stupid to pretend we can get anything back—"

For just a second I damned near spilled my real reason for being there—it seemed like I should warn her—have her prepared—but I knew she'd only hate me if I tried so I turned and walked out feeling small enough to walk under the screen door bottom without ducking my head.

I cut straight back past the gray outhouse east of the barn and was almost in the neighbor's yard when I heard a car behind me and turned around. The car came up the gravel drive beside Jenny's house and parked near the barn doors. It was a Buick. Nate got out and went into the house.

I still wasn't feeling tall when I reached the hotel and for a time I considered going straight to Boswell's for a bottle session but after a few seconds I went down to City Hall and walked in on Orrie who was smoking a cigar and glowering at his desk.

I wondered if he felt uneasy sitting in the chair where his deputy had died.

"Well?" he growled as I leaned against the doorjamb.

"You find out what killed Torky?" I asked.

"Doc says strychnine. What they use for rats. Almost enough in that bottle to kill you."

"I don't suppose there were any fingerprints?"

"Sure—yours and Torky's. What've you been up to?"

I leaned against his desk and told him I'd walked Jenny home.

"You planning to cut out her salesman?"

"I sure wouldn't mind. But I was wondering if Nate's been hanging around. When I left, he drove up. Could you find out if he's still working for the creamery in Loden?"

"Why should I?"

"If he quit—he must've had a good reason. Jobs ain't that easy to come by these days."

"You been looking?"

"You're funny as a boil on the glans—are you gonna check it out or aren't you?"

"A boil on the *what*?"

"Ass—you understand that?"

"Ass I always understand—but you didn't say ass."

"So I stutter—you gonna find out about Nate?"

He grumped around but finally called his cohort in Loden and asked him to check it out.

"Don't let on that I asked, though—just make it sound like you're curious—we don't want to rattle him yet."

The man agreed and at about nine when I drifted by Orrie's office he got the word. Nate had taken a week off—said his ma was sick and he had to go home and take care of her.

"Did Jenny look sick to you?" Orrie asked me.

"No," I said, "she was just fine."

"That's too bad," he said, shaking his head slowly. "I'd guess she's gonna be sick before long."

CHAPTER
13

After talking with Orrie I drifted down to Gus's Café, took a stool at the rear end of the counter and ordered a chocolate soda.

"Don't you dare spike it," said Rose.

"You poke your pinky in it and it'll have all the kick I need."

She said I was a nut and went to wait on a couple truck drivers. Gus was nowhere in sight so when Rose came near again I asked about him.

"His Mrs. says he's not feeling well."

"Had the doctor?"

"No." Rose grinned. "She says it's probably just the time for his change in life. You know—more like in the head." She spoke in low tones and tried to sound solemn but didn't have much luck.

"I know how that goes—puts a man off his feed."

"It seems like it's put Gus clear off his feet. He's been laying around for near a week now."

"He'd ought to go see Doc."

Rose shook her head. "I don't think she wants him to. She's afraid Doc won't find anything wrong and people'll figure Gus's just goofing off."

I'd finished all the soda and was working on the ice cream with a long-handled spoon. "So since when has the grand lady worried about what the mob thinks?"

"Everybody in Corden worries about what other people think—except maybe you."

I dug out the last of the ice cream, paid her a dime and walked up the hill to Gus's house. When I knocked on the door he didn't exactly drag himself to answer but he was a hell of a ways from frisky. I told him I'd heard he was sick and was dropping in for a visit. He invited me in as if I were an honest man and that convinced me he was in poor shape.

The living room shades, which had been drawn against the morning sun, were still down and we sat in the gloom—him in a big old Morris chair and me on the davenport which had enough give to sink me half out of sight. When I asked him what his trouble was he waved his arm wearily and said he was just run-down.

"It's lucky you've got Claire to take over the café."

"Yes," he agreed, without enthusiasm.

"I understand she'd been working there before—since about the first of the year. I suppose she got bored just taking care of the house, huh?"

"She got restless," he admitted.

"You think she ever wishes she'd stayed in politics?"

"She's never said so."

"I suppose she was pretty let-down when the judge didn't make governor. Did she really manage his campaign or was that just local talk?"

He stirred in the big chair and his eyes, which seemed too deeply sunk in his skull to see out, suddenly took on some life.

"She managed his campaign, all right. She did it very well. The trouble was, he never gave her much to work with—he was a cold man, very ineffective campaigner—"

"I heard he was a stuffed shirt."

"Well, that's the way he looked most of the time—"

"Did Claire want you in politics?"

94

He met my eyes for a moment and I thought he was going to ignore the question. Then he crossed his legs with an effort and tipped his head against the chair back.

"We talked about it in the early days—before we were married. There was a time, right after the judge lost, that she turned away from all of that completely, but pretty soon she got over it and I could tell that all the stuff still interested her more than anything else so of course I pretended I felt the same. You do that with women you want, don't you? Try to be what you think they'll admire?"

That wasn't my style but I knew what he meant and nodded.

"Ever take a flyer at running for office?" I asked.

"I went to caucuses and listened to some speeches and sat in on a few get-togethers. But I couldn't stand all of that wrangling and maneuvering. The very thought of actually running for election appalled me. All of that energy and struggle to get votes from people who'd never understand anything that was really going on ... I couldn't bear that final judgment, the choice between some other man and me by a great mass of people. Not even a small group. Could you stand that?"

It was a business I couldn't even think about but I shook my head to encourage him.

"You have to be a gambler or a masochist or mad— probably all three. It takes a rare conceit to expose yourself that way and expect to win. It surprises me, when I think about it, that it all fascinated Claire—she's never been a gambler. But money has never been that important to her—maybe because she never had to do without it. What she has is pride—she's always had that. Bitter pride."

"You figure you let her down?"

His head jerked forward and for an instant his deep eyes glared at me.

"I meant, because you didn't go into politics," I said.

He closed his eyes and tilted back again. "That. Yes, I suppose so. After all, I misrepresented myself in the beginning. But I doubt that she ever really believed I'd be a politician. Claire has few illusions."

"How'd she feel about Flory?"

He opened his eyes and gave me a little ironic smile.

"What do you mean—as a political candidate?"

I grinned. "No, as an employee."

"She thought she was a competent waitress, when she tended to business."

"Did she know you were in love with her?"

He stirred, unfolded his legs, leaned to one side until his left elbow was resting on the chair arm, and gave me a weary smile.

"What makes you think I was in love with that child?"

"A lot of things. The way you lost your temper when you saw her flirting with young guys, the fact her death has aged you ten years, and because Claire smiled when she saw you yell at the kid last winter."

"Who told you that?"

"You weren't alone in the café, Gus. There were lots of witnesses when you blew up."

"And all eager to talk, eh? Well, I *was* fond of Flory. Everybody was. She was pretty, gay, practically an orphan—you couldn't help but feel protective—and no one could feel innocent when she was murdered—not if they knew her well."

"What happened to her old man?"

"He was a bum. He walked out. One morning he left home for work—he did something at the courthouse—a clerk, I think—and they never heard from him again. Flory thought he just got fed up with his wife, who's a slattern. I don't mean she went with other men—she was too lazy—the house was always a shambles, meals were terrible. The minute Flory finished high school she left home and I don't think she's been back in her mother's house since."

"You think Flory hated her ma?"

"No, I wouldn't say that. It was more as if she feared her. I had the feeling that Flory thought if she stayed around home she'd become trapped in her mother's way of life. As if it were slough—or a disease."

"It sounds like you must've talked with her quite a bit."

He straightened up, folded his hands in his lap and stared at them.

"In a café, you're either working desperately or you're killing time. There were lots of afternoons when we sat around and talked—Rose, Joel, Flory and me."

"Dedee ever talk?"

"No. She has no conversation. She answers questions."

"How'd she like Flory?"

He thought about that for a moment. "That's strange— I've really no idea. Flory didn't pay her much attention. As a matter of fact, I think she rather deliberately avoided any sort of contact. Who knows? She may have felt a little about Dedee as she did about her own mother—as someone who could contaminate her with something that'd keep her from success."

"You figure Flory was ambitious?"

"Oh yes, absolutely. All of the fellows used to tell her she should go to Hollywood and while she pretended to laugh them off, I don't believe she thought it was ridiculous at all."

"She ever talk about her plans?"

He gave me a smile that was the saddest I've ever seen. He started to speak, swallowed, shook his head slowly and said, "No—except for one thing. She told us one day that she'd never die in Corden."

CHAPTER
14

I went from Gus's down to the pool hall, thinking I might find Nate around. Willie Norris talked me into playing snooker and in a little over an hour and a half I won four dollars from him. Nate didn't show.

Most of Corden had gone to bed by the time I walked home. The streets had a ghost-town look except for half a dozen cars parked in front and beside the hotel and a few more in front of the café. The movie had let out and in half an hour Gus's would close and the streets could be rolled up. Orrie's car wasn't in front of City Hall so I knew he was out taking a swing around town and making passes through all the lover's lanes. He wasn't the kind to sneak up with a flashlight but he liked to stop a little behind parked cars and shine his headlights on them. Usually they moved—a few waved. Those were the ones sitting up. He never got out and snooped but drove off after the light warning.

I went into his office and gave his desk a once-over, thinking he might have another love note about me, but didn't find anything. As I drifted back to the front door he pulled up and parked at the curb.

"How's the action?" I asked as he got out.

"Quiet as a lady's fart. What you been up to?"

I told him about my visit with Gus. He waddled past me,

nodding wisely, plunked down in his captain's chair and tilted it against the wall as he unwrapped a cigar.

"You don't seem too surprised about Gus," I said.

"Oh, I'm surprised enough—but mostly because he unloaded on you. He's always been a close man—I don't guess any man in town really knows him much. And he sounds like a sick man right now—I don't understand why he don't go see Doc."

"Rose figures his Mrs. doesn't want anybody to know Gus is just loafing. But I don't think that's it. You done anything to find out where the poison came from that was in the booze?"

"I asked Kiely if anybody bought anything from his drugstore—and checked Hokenson's Hardware about poisons. Neither of 'em remembers anybody buying anything like that lately."

"How about in Loden—could you check there?"

He squinted at me through cigar smoke.

"You really got Nate picked, eh?"

"He'd ought to be checked out."

"Yeah, that's what I figured. I already checked. Same story. I tried Parkersville and St. James and come up empty."

"You try Aquatown?"

"I don't know anybody there."

"They still got cops. You could call them."

"It wouldn't do any good. I'm a hay-shaker to them guys—and there's too many places and people in that town."

That sounded silly to me but I couldn't budge him.

"Okay," I said, "tomorrow I'll drive over there and check around myself—or are you gonna accuse me of skipping town if I leave?"

"Nobody's gonna tell you anything there."

"I won't know until I try."

He shrugged and said okay, damnit, go.

I pulled into Aquatown about 9:30 A.M. the next morning, parked on the main drag and meandered down to the drugstore on Maple and First. Things were quiet—a kid was sweeping the front walk, a woman was polishing spigots at the fountain and in back a squatty guy in a white coat fussed around drug shelves. I had a soda at the fountain, kidded the woman, who didn't respond, and after paying up, wandered over to the druggist. He'd been watching me off and on, side-eye style—and he made the study direct when I came near. My clothes were reasonably clean if not exactly immaculate and my pants had lost all memory of a press but I was clean-chinned and clear-eyed so he hadn't pegged me as a complete bum yet.

"Mr. Clinton?" I asked.

"That's me," he admitted.

It wasn't an ingenious identification—his name was on the front window and nobody else around would fit the bill. I gave him my all-out serious mug and explained I was doing a little work for the chief of police in Corden.

"We had a deputy poisoned yesterday—awful thing— you know? Second killing this month in our town. We figure there's a tie-in between 'em—"

His eyes got bright. "Sure—I read about that girl—head smashed—young kid—"

"You got it. Well listen—Officer Buford figures this deputy was on to whoever killed the girl—her name was Flory—and the killer poisoned him. Now we're pretty sure the poison didn't come from our area or near—so we're checking here—can you help us out?"

He would be absolutely tickled pink. It was too bad because when he checked records and we talked with his people, nothing came up.

I drifted down the street a block and went into a hardware store. The place was empty except for a woman halfway down the center aisle. She was checking an order sheet clipped to a small board. All I could see was the top of her head, which was covered with rich brown hair. When I stopped about a yard away she looked up and took me in with big brown eyes behind rimless glasses. Her gaze was hawk sharp.

"Hi," I said, "I don't suppose you're the boss here?"

"Why not?" Her voice was husky.

"No reason," I admitted, "only I never saw a lady working in a hardware store, let alone running one."

"Well, you never saw me before."

I couldn't argue that so I grinned as innocent as I can and went through my spiel about working for Orrie Buford. She kept looking me over while I talked, as if she were planning to make a good description to the cops at a future date. I returned the study, finding that she was slim without being bony, a little over five foot tall and probably not much over thirty years old.

"You got any identification?" she asked when I ran down.

"What do you want identification for?"

"So I know you're who you say you are."

"I haven't got a badge, if that's what you want to know— all I'm asking is did a guy or a woman come in here and buy anything to kill rats—or anything else—with?"

She took off her glasses and gave me a good look at her dark, heavy eyebrows and sharp brown eyes with whites as pure as fresh snow. I hardly noticed the tiny crow's feet at the corners.

"If you're not a real officer or deputy, how come you're doing police work?"

"I'm a volunteer—public spirited."

She gave me a cool look. "Uh-huh. And this girl—was she something special to you?"

"She worked in my old man's hotel—but she wasn't my girlfriend, if that's what you're getting at."

"How about the deputy—was he a friend?"

"As a matter of fact, I didn't like him much. And since it seems I'm not going to get any questions answered till I dump my life story—I want to find the real killer so nobody pins this thing on me—okay?"

"Why'd anybody want to pin it on you?"

"Well, one reason is I'm the only ex-con in Corden."

"Ah," she said, and nodded. "What'd you go to prison for?"

"I worked for a lady who needed more cattle than she could buy. The fella that owned them was selfish and sent some guys to crimp the show and I got caught when my horse stepped in a gopher hole and broke his leg. That cost me a year."

In case you're wondering, I told her about the rustling instead of the jewelry store stickup because it seemed more wholesome.

She watched me with her big brown eyes and finally said, "You wouldn't be kidding me a little, would you?"

"No."

She shook her head. "I can't imagine a fellow like you being that stupid."

"What do you mean, a fella like me?"

She grinned a little. "I'm not too sure—how'd your nose get broken?"

"It got in the way of a guy's boot."

She folded her arms under her small breasts and leaned back against the counter. "I suppose you drink."

"On occasion—don't you?"

"I have—but I never let it make a fool of me."

"Well, bully for you."

She laughed. "You're something, you are. All right, someone broke in here a week ago on the weekend. He took all the money from the till, a .38-caliber pistol, a Remington shotgun, eight boxes of shells and one box of rat poison. I noticed the poison because I'd only had two on the shelf at the time—an order I placed was late coming in."

"When was this?"

"A week ago Saturday night—sometime after closing Saturday and opening Monday morning."

"How'd he get in?"

"Jimmied the lock in the alley. It wasn't too hard. We never been robbed before. The next one won't find it so easy."

"I bet he won't. What's your name?"

"Angela Wynters—with a wye. And nobody calls me Angie."

"You a widow?"

"That's right. Husband owned this place—I took over when he went to war. He died of flu so I kept on. I'm the only woman running a hardware store in South Dakota. Maybe in the whole Midwest."

I offered to roll her a cigarette and she said okay and watched while I built two. When we were both set I lit hers, then mine and we stood there, letting the smoke float off while we looked each other over some more.

"You got the serial numbers for the guns stolen?" I asked.

"Sure. You have any notion who the fellow is?"

"Just a notion—no proof."

She took short puffs on the cigarette and squinted against the rising smoke.

I grinned at her. "You don't smoke much, do you?"

"No," she admitted, and looked at the cigarette doubtfully.

"How come you took that one?"

"I just never tried a hand-rolled one before."

"How many factory mades have you tried?"

"Not many—why?"

"I just get a kick out of a woman willing to try something different. You're a pretty special woman, you know that?"

"Some think I work pretty hard at it." She laughed again. It was, I decided, a sound I'd like to hear often.

"How about when I get this killing thing squared away— how about I come back and tell you what happened?"

"Will you come sober?"

"Mostly."

"All right, sure. I'd like that just fine."

"Great—I'll hurry."

CHAPTER
15

The lobby thermometer had edged past 100 degrees before noon the next day and you couldn't see straight across the gravel road for the squiggly heat waves that distorted everything like a cheap mirror. Old Elihu sat in his swivel chair with his collar open and his coat off, smoking a La Fendrich he could have lit on the sidewalk out front. A couple sparrows perched on the bumper of a Model A Ford, waiting for grasshoppers on the radiator to finish baking. Or maybe they were just too heat-pooped to fly up and peck.

I sat in a rocker, daydreaming of the hardware lady. She was the first widow I'd met who didn't need help and I was trying to convince myself this was a sign that things were going to take new directions for Carl Wilcox. Maybe I could work out something—provide a delivery service— help run the place. Hardware stores have always been toyland to me—I'd rather be turned loose in one than any grocery, clothing or general store there ever was. Imagine helping yourself to any tool, fishing gear, gadget or knife that you wanted—I guess it'd even beat a liquor store. What a combination—a fine woman and a hardware store—it was worth dreaming about.

"I hear," said Elihu, "that old Gus is bad off. Doc went up there this morning."

"Hear what's wrong?"

"I don't think Dōc knows. He just looks wise and solemn."

I went up for a visit. Claire answered my knock and frowned through the screen at me.

I asked how Gus was.

"Right now he's sleeping. What do you want?"

I smiled at her. "What're you offering?"

She tried to smile back, had trouble with it, and after a couple seconds said, "I could offer you iced tea."

"I'd take it."

The blinds were drawn on the south side and a fan hummed on the floor in the hall. Another fan worked in the living room. I sat on a flowered sofa and stared at a landscape painting on the north wall until Claire returned carrying two glasses on a small round tray.

The fact that she was treating me like acceptable society told me so much I decided to challenge her but first I went through the motions and stirred sugar into the tea, making the ice clink against the glass. It was a lovely, cool sound.

"I'll tell Gus you called," she said.

"That'll resurrect him like Lazarus."

She didn't smile or frown—it was as though I hadn't said anything. She just watched me.

"What did you want to see him about?" she asked.

In the soft light she looked no more than twenty and tragic as Garbo only not so noble.

I tested the tea, took a good swallow and leaned back.

"To tell you the truth, I didn't really expect to see Gus. I heard he was in a bad way and wondered if maybe you'd be home, looking after him."

"Well, you see I am."

"Uh-huh. What I wondered most about was which was more important—the café or Gus."

"The café can take care of itself."

"Yup, it always could, with Rose and Joel around. So why'd you have to go down and take charge last January?"

She considered me with her hazel eyes for a long moment, then shook her head. "I can't think of any reason why I should answer your questions."

I grinned at her. "That's two of us—but you have been. So how come you invited me in, why've you talked with me before? Why is Claire Gardner being polite to Carl Wilcox?"

"Because I'm probably less of a snob than you are, and I'm trying to be as civilized as possible with whomever comes to my house for whatever reason."

"You do just fine, Mrs. Gardner, and if you'll let me take advantage of all your civilization, I'd like to give you a nutshell version of some things I've figured out—okay?"

"About what?"

"Flory's murder."

She stared at me for a second, then, with no expression at all, said, "Go ahead."

"Okay—this is all pretty rough and sloppy—but be patient. Now, everybody knows Gus has always had a weakness for young girls—nothing clumsy—he pats them on the shoulder, not the fanny, watches them close but makes it look like sympathy, not lust, and generally plays the understanding daddy. That fed your contempt but you could be tolerant because it wasn't bad enough to make folks pity the wife. Then, last winter, you got a clue that Gus had fallen for a real live one—a kid with looks, some brains and a lot of ambition—and she was encouraging Gus. So you went down to the café to 'help out' and saw what was happening right off. Gus was scared spitless when you took over—he knew damned well you'd figured things out—and you rubbed it in by showing Flory how strong you are and how weak poor Gus is. Gus knew he'd never have another chance for hanky-panky and it got him so worked up he finally lost his head and bawled Flory out in front of a crowd—showing himself up as a jealous lover. And by making a fool of himself, he made a fool of you. That's where the tolerance stopped. You decided to get rid of her."

Claire's eyes were steady on mine as she held her iced tea glass just over her skirted knees. The ice was nearly melted.

"It took a while to arrange," I went on, "because Corden isn't a town where you can hire people to murder without stirring up a hell of a lot of talk. But all of a sudden, one night, Nate is in town, drunk and mad—and best of all— he's mad at Flory. All you have to do is find a way for him to come on her while she's alone and he's drunk and mean. That's where I'm having the most trouble—I figure somehow you got a note to Flory asking her to meet Gus behind the hotel—maybe you'd worked it out of Gus that he'd planned to run off with her—"

Claire brought the iced tea to her lips, sipped slowly and continued watching me.

"When Flory came out of the hotel to meet Gus, she found Nate and it was checkout time. I'd guess it was Nate's idea to pin the rap on me—but maybe you suggested it—old politicians don't forget what happens between people when it might be useful later. Then, when it looked like I wasn't only wriggling off the hook but was maybe going to be a nuisance—you fixed up a little personalized moonshine and Nate made the special delivery. That I figure was strictly your idea. Women have always liked poison over blunt instruments. I keep trying to picture your talks with Nate—they must've been something. He's not the kind to get himself in a plot with a good-looking woman and overlook the bedding chances. That's one thing I don't think you'd do—I'd guess you'd rather lay with a tarantula."

She put her glass on the end table beside her chair and gave me a chilly smile.

"I'm glad you have such a high opinion of me—not only my morals, but my attractiveness. I don't know how I feel about the young man—I don't even know what he looks like—and I've never spoken to him. Have you had enough tea?"

"Yeah." I put the glass down and had a sudden notion that putting anything in my mouth in her house might not be too brilliant. On the other hand it wasn't too likely she'd let me have it in her living room since then she'd have to haul the body out herself. I wasn't altogether comforted by those thoughts because she was one hell of a resourceful woman.

She stood up and smoothed her skirt down.

"Do you have anything else you want to tell me?"

"Not just now. A couple things are shaping up though— I'll keep you posted."

"Do. Especially about how I lured Flory out to her rendezvous with death—and where I had meetings with— what's his name? Nate?"

I told her I'd drop in again when Gus was feeling better and she said that'd be lovely. We were so polite it about made me sick.

I hiked down toward town trying to figure out what made her so damned smug. The more I puzzled it over the surer I was that her contact with Nate was the key. There was no problem with how she'd known what happened in the Playhouse—she could always overhear talk like that in the café—but if she talked directly with Nate there, someone would have noticed and gossiped about it. If she talked to him anytime after the killing, it would have had to be done secretly and where in hell could she manage that in Corden? Obviously she hadn't made the contact herself—it had to be through a hired hand. It wasn't likely

Rose, she couldn't keep her mouth shut thirty seconds, it probably wasn't Joel, he was too close to Gus. That left Dedee. She wasn't very bright, to put it generously, but she'd follow any orders Claire gave and she sure as hell wouldn't blab. Also it wasn't likely she'd ever put two and two together if strange things happened after her notes or messages were delivered.

I walked slowly along the baking sidewalk and squinted against the sun's glare. The sky was open blue, burned thin by the naked fire and there wasn't enough breeze to tilt a tumbleweed.

Gus's Café seemed cool and heavenly and I stood inside the door, blinking through the comparative darkness while the overhead fans turned lazily, hardly making a hum. The place was empty except for Rose, Joel and Dedee, all sitting in the booth next to the kitchen door in back. They watched in silence as I walked the length of the café and stopped beside them. Joel and Dedee had root beers, Rose was drinking coffee.

"It figures," I said, "the boss is gone so all the help starts drinking up the profits."

Rose and Joel smiled but they weren't that amused. It was a hell of a polite day. I asked for a cup of coffee and Dedee got up to pour it for me. She was a little girl with pigeon toes, slim ankles and a poor complexion. Brown bangs flopped across her forehead, almost hiding the acne, but there was nothing she could do about the rest except when she was sitting down. Then she cupped her face with both hands leaving only the little nose and the blue eyes exposed. She didn't sit down after getting me coffee but went to fuss behind the counter, polishing something.

I nodded toward her and said, "There's a good kid."

"Yeah," agreed Joel, "but who likes kids?"

"How old is she?"

"Why? You know if they're big enough they're old enough."

I shook my head. "That's marvelous. I never thought of it quite that way. You got a fantastic mind, Joel."

Sarcasm slipped off him like snow off a hot radiator.

"I know, I know." He grinned.

"She's older'n she looks," said Rose. "I heard once but I forgot."

"She's been working here five years, right?" I asked.

"Yeah, about. She quit school soon's they'd let her—never graduated."

"How'd Gus happen to hire her—wasn't she hard to train?"

"Gus wouldn't've hired her," said Joel. "Mrs. Gardner talked him into it."

Rose nodded. "Her ma worked for the judge—she was his housekeeper for years. Dedee was the old lady's only kid and when she was ready to work, Mrs. Gardner said Gus would find something for her. Gus put her to doing dishes and cleaning off tables but pretty soon she was able to serve tables too and now she does about everything."

"Yeah," said Joel, "she's not good at any of it, but she does it all."

Dedee guessed we were talking about her and I could see her scarred face getting pink. Pretty soon she walked out to the kitchen. I got up and trailed her. She looked spooked when she saw it was me but when I grinned and asked if it was okay if I looked around at where all the good grub came from, she nodded shyly.

"How's your ma?" I asked. "She still working for the judge?"

"Huh-uh. Ma died."

"Golly—that's too bad—when'd that happen?"

"While you was in prison."

I shook my head. "A lot happened that year—sometimes I think I'll never get caught up."

The blue eyes darted around the kitchen, then suddenly met my gaze and fixed steadily. "What was it like—there?"

"It was mostly tiresome, Dedee."

She nodded, vaguely unbelieving. "Did they—did they beat on you?"

"No—why'd they do that?"

" 'Cause you'd been bad."

"Go on—I wasn't that bad."

"Then why'd they put you in prison?"

"Oh, I see what you mean—yeah, they put me there because I'd been bad—but see—once you get in there you sort of start fresh. They don't much care what you'd done as long as you don't cause any trouble in the place. I stayed sober and didn't get in trouble so nobody hit me."

"Did they put you in the hole?"

"No—I told you—I stayed out of trouble. How come you ask, Dedee—where'd you hear about the hole?"

She looked toward the back door. "It just seems like a awful thing, to be put in a—a place like that."

She was like my ma—figured if you avoided words that named bad things they were less real and wouldn't touch you.

"I wasn't so crazy about it I plan to go back," I admitted, "but how'd you hear so much about prison?"

Her mouth got tight and I could feel her withdrawing.

"Is it okay to smoke out here?" I asked.

She said Joel did so that made it okay and I rolled and lit one. I said I understood she'd worked at the café for over five years and that I guessed she probably knew by now what everybody like to eat. She nodded.

"What's Orrie ask for when he drops by at night?"

"Apple pie à la mode and coffee."

"How about the judge—he comes in now and then—?"

"Scoop of ice cream—vanilla—no chocolate."

"What's Lard like?"

"Hot fudge sundae."

"How about Nate?"

"Cherry pie à la mode."

I said I guessed she'd waited on all of them lots of times and she nodded. I asked if they were all nice to her. She shrugged.

"Any of them talk to you?"

Her expression became guarded. "Some," she admitted.

"How about the night before last—did Nate talk to you any?"

"No," she said. She picked up a washcloth and began rubbing out a stain on the serving table. Her mouth twisted to one side as she applied pressure and the tip of her pink tongue showed in the pulled corner. I guessed she was enjoying the questions but was a little afraid about giving answers. She wasn't used to much attention. It was a little like trying to soothe a spooked pony and I tried to sound especially casual when I asked the most important question.

"You ever see Nate talking with Mrs. Gardner?"

Her eyes became round as she looked up at me and then Joel appeared in the dining room entrance and said Dedee was wanted on the telephone.

Dedee's eyes went wider than ever. "For me?"

"Yeah, yeah—it's Mrs. Gardner so get a wiggle on—she ain't gonna wait all day."

Dedee gave me a terrified look and darted out. I followed and saw her snatch up the receiver and stand on tiptoe to bring her mouth close to the wall telephone. Within a few seconds she had hung up and was hurrying toward the street door.

"Hey!" yelled Joel. "Where the hell you think you're going?"

113

"To Mrs. Gardner's—"

And she was gone.

I went back to the booth and sat down with Rose. Joel tromped into the kitchen, looking annoyed.

"That happen often?" I asked.

"Not very."

"But it's not unusual?"

"Dedee's Mrs. Gardner's personal hired girl. When Mrs. Gardner calls, Dedee comes—and she's tickled to death. She loves that house and all the fancy things—you know there's a dollhouse in the guest room all furnished down to silverware, chandeliers and carpets? I've never seen it but Dedee's told me—it must really be lovely—"

"Does Dedee have a love life?"

"Oh my no—she's scared of fellas—they make her all walleyed and fidgety."

"Don't any of the fellas make a play?"

"Well, Nate talks to her some. You know him, he'll try for anything in a skirt. I think she kinda likes him—nobody else notices her hardly and he always talks nice—no smart-aleck stuff or treating her like a child. She can tell right away when people do that. In some ways, Dedee's not as dumb as you'd think."

She brought me another cup of coffee, poured one for herself and sat down again.

"Ever see Nate use the telephone here?" I asked.

"I don't remember any time—why?"

"I'm just a nosy bastard—you think you'd notice if he did?"

"About the only thing I notice about Nate is that when he's drunk he's mean and he pinches. I don't know or care if he uses the telephone."

I kept at her but she began getting suspicious and uneasy and started asking more questions than she answered. After a while I gave up and went over to City Hall for a chinning session with Orrie.

He sat in his captain's chair, tilted against the wall and tried to cool himself by waving a dinky cardboard fan with an ad for Larson's Grocery. It took more energy than he could spare in the heat and despite the dry he was able to produce a fair amount of sweat.

I told him about my day's work. He let the chair flop to all four legs and stopped fanning about halfway through my account of the dialogue with Claire. Pretty soon he was shaking his head.

"Jesus Christ. Jesus H. Christ—you just up and laid it out, right to her face?"

"Why not?"

He thought that over, shrugged and tilted his chair back again.

"What'd she say?"

"She asked if I'd like more tea."

"I'll be damned. You had the guts to drink tea she poured?"

"Not after my speech. And I've got it figured how she made connections with Nate. It was through Dedee. That kid's putty in Claire's hands—she'd do anything for her. Everybody's putty in that woman's hands—she's even got Nate being polite to Dedee—or at least acting human enough not to scare her."

"Huh! Well, if she did manage it all, you sure as hell showed her how smart you are—but damned if I see the good of it. What the hell did you expect? A confession?"

"I figured I'd rattle her—that she'd naturally start to argue—you know—pick holes—and maybe make a mistake."

"Uh-huh. You were trying to impress her—that's what. And that was dumb. She's a hell of a ways too smart for you and me put together."

The hell of it was, I knew he was right.

CHAPTER
16

Ⅰ decided to visit Lil. No doubt Orrie had already questioned her but being a cop he wouldn't talk her language and being a bum I figured I did.

Lil wasn't very professional. She never had a pimp, didn't set regular rates and operated only when she was in the mood—which usually could be brought on by a bottle of booze and a randy man. Early in her career I'd taken my turn because I'd heard she did it for pure fun and like every other damned fool kid I figured nothing could be sweeter than a roll in the hay with a woman who loved getting laid and didn't give a damn for getting married or worrying what folks would say.

The house, which her old man left her God knows how long before, was at the upper northwest edge of town. From the front step she could look across the valley and take in the Catholic cemetery a bit to the south and the Protestant graveyard to the north. Straight east her attic window offered a fine view of the county's deepest sandpit which had been abandoned for at least five years. Corden was south but on the slope covered with elms, box elders and cottonwoods you couldn't see much more than leaves and patches of roof during the summer.

The front walk sprouted weeds from all the cracks and was surrounded by untrimmed grass. I ambled up to the stoop which had no approach steps and hopped up to cross the creaking porch.

A tap on the screen door brought Lil down the hall from the kitchen, walking slow and easy. She wore a button-front purple housedress with short sleeves, pink mules and a wise grin. Bleached hair curled around her face, which was full-lipped, pug-nosed and a little slant-eyed.

"Well, well, look who's here—old busted-face Carl Wilcox! You come up for dinner, Carl?"

"That's all you're offering these days?"

"I'm open to offers—what're you after?"

"All I can get and a little extra."

"So what'd you bring me?"

I patted my hip. "Some of Boswell's best."

"His best is none too good," she said, but she pushed the door open. Her perfume, sweet and strong, didn't quite cover the scent of animal as I passed close to her and stepped into the hall.

"Go into the living room," she said, "I'll get us glasses."

Like everyone else in Corden during the summer Lil had all the green shades drawn flush with the sill so the room was dark and stuffy. I pulled the pint flask from my hind pocket, parked it on the side table and sat down on the rosy sofa. A picture of Lil's old man scowled at me from beside the pint and I reached over to lay him facedown. I can't stand being stared at by a man without a sense of humor.

Lil came in through the dining room and for half a second light from the kitchen went through the thin cotton dress giving me a glimpse of her silhouette. She had sturdy legs, round hips and a waist just beginning to thicken but still trim enough to make lines I like.

"You haven't been around for a long time," she said, accusingly.

"I haven't had a bottle in a long time."

"Huh! You've had all too damned many from what I hear.

And been to prison since I saw you last. Maybe you hadn't ought to have any of this."

"Don't start talking like my old lady, pour."

She did and then raised her glass. "Here's to hell, may the stay there match the way there."

I drank to that and for a moment we were still after she'd sat down beside me and we listened to the grandfather clock, ticking hollowly in the corner across from us. I looked around the room and shook my head.

"It's amazing," I said.

"What?"

"The way you keep this place so neat. I can't picture you charging around the house with dust rags, mops and brooms."

"I don't charge around at anything. Everything Lil does, she does nice and easy." She propped her elbow on the sofa arm and gave me her wide, toothy grin. "I do it all at night—after I've had company I'm restless—got to be doing something—so I clean the joint." She giggled. "Some of the guys that stay—they think I'm crazy. That's the ones that stay awake long enough to notice."

I tried to remember if I'd stayed awake but it had been a fuzzy night a long time ago and if I had, any activities following the main event had been blissfully slept through.

"You pretty much follow your own drummer, don't you?"

"I don't follow nothing or nobody," she said, and pushed her glass at me for another slug. She sipped, tilted her head back and smoothed the lines in her neck. "You look skinnier than when I saw you last—didn't they feed you at Stillwater?"

"Every meal fit for a tramp. I'm not skinnier, just older."

"Getting older doesn't make me look skinnier," she said. "Just sexier."

"Yeah? If I look so sexy, why're you so slow?"

118

"I'm like you, Lil, I try to take things nice and easy. Why—you in a hurry to start cleaning house?"

"No, but I cook after I clean and I'm already getting hungry."

"Fine—let's eat."

She accepted that and led me out to the kitchen where in no time she whipped up ham and eggs with hashed brown potatoes, sliced tomatoes and coffee. The potatoes were greasy and the coffee was strong enough to fight Dempsey but you can't expect Ritz meals in a one-woman whore-house so I downed it all and complemented the cook as we relaxed with smokes. Lil leaned her elbows on the table and frowned at me.

"Okay—what're you really after?"

"What the hell do you mean? What'd I be after but the usual?"

"Come on—the usual hasn't been usual with you in years and you're acting coy as a virgin cowhand and stalling like a Scotchman in front of a pay toilet. If you're after money—I haven't got any—and you can't borrow any or take it either."

"Jesus Christ—you think I came up here to rob you?"

"Well, you sure ain't set on rape and you've been up the river twice for robbery, haven't you?"

"Never. Once for *attempted* robbery, and the other time for rustling—and both times it was *for* women—not *from* them."

"Rustling's just another kind of robbery—only more trouble than money—how could you be so damned dumb, Carl?"

"I wasn't dumb—I was drunk."

"So what d'ya want from me? The grandfather clock? I noticed you studying it in there."

"No—a watch is too much handier. Goddamnit, Lil, if

you're gonna be snotty, let's go to bed and see if that helps your disposition."

"Well," she said, getting up, "I thought you'd never ask."

Actually I had a good time. It'd been a hell of a while between rounds and all my eager turned Lil so active and acrobatic that twice I lost contact after making good connections and that made her move so fast it started me laughing and I damned near lost my starch. The first time it made her mad, the second time she laughed too and we about fell off the bed.

Afterward she cleaned us both up and started to put on her dress but I told her the house was already indecently clean and pulled her back to bed. When she found I wasn't ready yet for round two she relaxed and let me just cozy up. The bed was right next to the open northside window which let a little breeze come through under the blind and we hardly noticed it was about 90 degrees in the shade.

She was half asleep when I asked if Nate came around often.

"You mean Jenny's boy?" she asked drowsily.

"Yeah. I heard he comes around every week."

She pulled her head away from my shoulder, propped her head up on a pillow and looked at me sleepily. "Yeah—he comes about that—when he gets to town. He really likes me."

"Does he bring you a bottle?"

"Mostly he brings lots of eager. He's, you know—greedy. Especially when he's not too drunk. 'Course, most of the time he's pretty drunk, but he always likes me. He says I'm the best there is."

"Is that right—"

I didn't sound convinced, I guess, because she gave me a frown and sat up.

"Yes, that's right. And he's brought me flowers. He brought me a whole dozen roses—"

"I'll be damned."

"Well, why shouldn't he?" she demanded. "And when I pricked my finger on one of the thorns, he even washed it for me—"

I tried to look gullible enough to swallow that but she'd stopped looking me in the eye so my act wasn't tested.

"When was that?" I asked.

"About two weeks ago—Saturday night."

"Was he drunk?"

"Oh boy—I'll say he was drunk. He could hardly see—I wasn't sure whether he'd get sick or go to sleep first but he was heading both ways. There were a couple fellas here and they kept kidding him but he just acted like they weren't around—"

"And he brought you roses and washed your thumb when it bled?"

She looked at me quickly, trying to remember what she'd said. "Yeah—that's right—only it was my finger I pricked."

"Uh-huh—you know where the prick is every time, right?"

She laughed and gave me a shove. I shoved her back and she grabbed me and pretty soon we were busy again only more slow and I kept wondering how in the hell I had managed to live through so many days without doing this each one. I wanted to keep at it until Christmas and then suddenly it was done and a few minutes later I was trying to decide how to get back to questions.

"What happened after Nate washed your finger?" I asked.

Lil reached over and ran her finger across my bumpy nose.

"What was this like before you got it busted?"

"I don't know—that was so long ago I've forgotten."

"You mean you were just a kid? How old?"

"Eight."

"How'd you get the hole in your chin?"

"That's not a hole, that's a dimple."

"Dimples are in cheeks."

"Not mine. What happened after Nate doctored your thumb?"

"What the hell do you care?"

"I'm trying to settle a bet, damnit."

She pinched my nose and flopped back down on the bed.

"Actually something funny did happen—not funny ha ha—just strange. He got a telephone call. One of the fellas answered and said it was for Nate. Nate didn't believe him at first but finally he took it and the next thing I knew he was hightailing it out the front door."

"What time was that?"

"I dunno—somewhere near midnight I suppose."

"What was the name of the guy who answered the phone?"

"Jeff Catton—works for Bower—drives a truck. Why?"

I gave her a squeeze and got up to dress. Lil propped both pillows behind her tousled head and scowled at me. "Why all the questions—what're you after?"

"I'll let you know when I find out. And next time I come, I'll bring a quart and flowers without thorns—okay?"

She grinned. "Lovely—you come any old time, Carl."

"And every time," I promised. "See you—"

CHAPTER
17

In the morning I found Catton was out of town on a truck run and wouldn't be back until the next day. I made the mistake of going back to the hotel where Ma latched on to me and next I was carrying out waste cans from the upstairs back apartments and burning papers in the fifty-five-gallon drum set about half a rod from where Flory had died in the backyard. I'd worked more than halfway through the junk when Orrie came out the shed door and waddled over.

"For God's sake, ain't it hot enough without you adding?"

"I figure to start a draft that'll pull cold air right from the North Pole."

He shifted his cigar from the left corner of his mug to the right and glared at the flames in the barrel.

"You ain't gonna believe what I'm gonna tell you," he said.

"Gimme a try."

"Gus Gardner just confessed to killing Flory."

"I don't believe you."

"Well, you'd better. He gimme a dying statement—and then he died."

"He say why he killed her?"

"He said he was her lover and it was his fault she was dead."

"It was his fault? But did he tell you he took that pipe and beat her head in?"

"That's exactly what I asked—and it was hard for him— he fought it and finally he said yes, he done it. He said he didn't mean to, it just somehow happened—he must've gone crazy. I asked where did he get the pipe and he said it was just laying there—he happened across it."

"How'd he know she'd be out there?"

"Look, it's one thing to take a dying statement from a man and it's a whole other thing to come around asking smart questions when you weren't there seeing a man like Gus telling something as awful as what he done—"

"How'd he explain planting the piece of pipe in my truck?"

"I never got to ask him that, Jesus—he was goin' too fast—"

"How'd he explain trying to poison me?"

"He said he didn't have nothing to do with that. I asked him that one and he swore there was no connection. He didn't have a single hard word to say about you, Carl."

"How'd you happen by for this deathbed scene?"

"His wife, Claire—she called me. She said hurry, he was going—I got over quick and she was there with Doc and he asked them to go out in the hall and he just talked to me alone there."

"When you knew he was making a confession, didn't you want witnesses?"

"Goddamnit, Carl—it's no easy thing listening to a dying man you've known all your life telling you he killed a girl like that. He just spilled it out like vomit—it wasn't like we was sitting in the office at City Hall where I could think everything out. I couldn't believe what I was hearing—and I sure as hell didn't want Claire in there—"

We stood and watched the flames in the oil drum work down to barely a flicker and didn't talk. Orrie, I guessed, was trying first to think of a good explanation for the planted evidence and then he got busy being sore at me for raising questions he should have asked and neither line made him feel chatty. Finally he allowed that the truck probably had just seemed a likely spot to stash the pipe.

"In a panic," he explained, "people do funny things."

"You honest to God believe that Gus Gardner picked up a piece of pipe off the ground in the dark, knocked Flory down and then pounded her head to mush, walked over to my truck, unfolded a blanket that was rolled behind the seat, put the pipe in it, put it back, walked home and slept?"

"How the hell do I know did he sleep? All I know is the man made a deathbed confession and that's good as gold, Goddamnit. You'd ought to be tickled pink he did it—it gets you off the hook."

"If you swallow it, I suppose you're right."

The town buzzed all afternoon and in the evening I went over to Boswell's and lifted a few. A fair breeze had come up after dusk and we sat in front of his shack, facing the railroad tracks and watching heat lightning flicker off to the west.

"Why'd Gus say he done it if he didn't?" Boswell asked me.

"Damned if I know. Maybe he just figured it was his fault, no matter who really did it. It's a damned funny thing that he'd get sick the way he did, when he did. When I talked to him last, he didn't seem to give a shit whether he lived or died."

"You think he killed himself some way?"

"No—not by inches like that."

Boswell got up, went inside and brought the jug out to refill our glasses.

"You figure Claire was slipping him something?"

"Yeah, I do. And I think he knew it and took it."

Boswell sat down, set the jug between us and shook his head. "It's too blamed mixed up for me," he confessed.

"It sure as hell isn't crystal clear to me."

By 7:30 the next morning I was over at Bower's place and located Jeff Catton gassing up his truck for another trip. He said he'd already had coffee but wouldn't mind one on me and we drifted over to Ted's counter shop across the street.

"I see Gus's place is closed this morning," he said, "I wonder if it'll ever open again."

Ted brought us coffee in white mugs and I lifted mine to Jeff who acknowledged it with a nod before taking a sip. It missed boiling by about half a degree and we both put our mugs on the counter.

Jeff was nearly as big as Lard but leaner and a lot older—probably about forty. His hair was thinning in front and gone at the crown but was still all dark except for white dandruff flecks. His left arm was tanner than the right and he wore a cut-off-sleeved shirt open at the collar. His hard-used face was brown, dry and sharp-jawed.

I wasn't too sure how to start the talk—Jeff was enough married so he might not be too crazy about admitting visits to Lil. He watched me close, his pale blue eyes alert and some defensive, but he grinned easy enough.

"I guess Gus's confession must've been good news for you, eh?" he said.

"Not especially—Orrie knew I didn't do it—and I knew it—so there wasn't all that much to worry about."

He shook his head. "A lot of folks thought different."

"How about you?"

He grinned. "I never figured punching out girls was your style, Carl."

"I appreciate that. Listen, we got a mutual friend up on

126

the hill—I understand you were there when a certain party got telephoned up there a couple weeks ago."

"Who, me?"

I let him waltz it around for a while but pretty soon he admitted he'd taken a call and finally he said yeah, it was a girl.

"Was it Dedee?"

His eyes opened wide. "How the hell'd you know that?"

"I didn't know it—but it seemed likely."

"Yeah? How in hell'd she know he'd be up there and how come she called even if she did? I mean, even say she was sweet on Nate, which seems to be the style with a lot of dumb women in this town, I never figured she had gumption enough to say boo to a goose—but here she calls a whorehouse in the middle of the night and asks for a guy!"

"What'd she say?"

"First she asked was I Nate. I said no and she says let me talk to him. I asked who's calling and she told me. That was a jolt—I sure's hell didn't want anybody like her to know I was at Lil's—so I called Nate and got the hell off the phone."

"Then what?"

"Nate got on and I went into the kitchen after a drink and when I came back, Nate was gone. Just hung up the phone and took off like a goosed duck."

"What time was that?"

"Some past midnight. How come you want to know about Nate—didn't Gus admit he killed Flory?"

"That's what you told me a few minutes ago."

"You don't figure he did it, huh?"

"I don't know what to think—I'm just trying to fit it together."

He gazed at me for a few seconds, then looked into his

coffee. "You won't be telling about me being up there, will you?"

"No."

He grinned. "Good—you could get me in real trouble."

"I wouldn't want that."

He slapped my shoulder and slid off the stool. "You're okay, Wilcox, I always said so. Suppose you'll be drifting again soon, eh?"

"I hadn't given it much thought."

"Sure, you'll go. You always have—I bet you always will. Too much of the Gypsy—place like Corden can't hold you. I'd guess every real man in town envies you some—you know—the bachelor—free as a Goddamned hawk. Sometimes I think I should have been like that—never got married and all nailed down . . ."

"You don't act much nailed down."

"Yeah—not enough—but I should. That takes the pleasure away—you know? Always worrying about hurting her and the kids—"

He wanted it all, like everybody else, and didn't have any notion of what he already had. I supposed it wasn't that much. I thanked him and he thanked me and we went our ways.

Over at City Hall I asked Orrie what he'd have to do to get a search warrant for Nate's place in Loden.

"What in hell'd I want a search warrant for?" he demanded.

"I think it'd be interesting to find a pistol and a shotgun and maybe a can of rat poison in Nate's room."

"That's too damned much of a long shot—I don't think I could get the warrant if I wanted it."

"And you don't want it?"

"It wouldn't do any good. And then Nate'd know you

128

were after his hide and if he did have the stuff he'd ditch it."

"I don't believe Nate'd ditch a slingshot, let alone a gun."

"Well, forget about a search warrant—the cop in Loden is a personal friend of Jack Wortle—Nate's boss."

"Well, fine—then how the hell do you plan to wrap this thing up?"

"As far as anybody's concerned but you, it is all wrapped up. Gus confessed—that's it."

"And you don't give a damn who tried to kill me and did kill your deputy?"

"Sure I give a damn—but it ain't gonna help Torky for me to go asking a Loden judge for a warrant to search Nate's place when I know damn well nobody's going to swallow your notions about somebody robbing a hardware store in Aquatown—which is a good sixty miles east of Loden. For Christ's sake, Carl—think about it a minute—it don't make any sense at all."

"It makes more sense than you've got. Okay, the hell with it. If you don't care, why the hell should I?"

"You care 'cause you got a hard-on for Nate because he spoiled your thing with Jenny."

We glared at each other for a while and then I asked did he plan to have an autopsy on Gus?

"What for?"

"To find out what killed him."

"Hell, nothing killed him—he just died. Doc was there, he'd know."

"What'd he say caused it?"

"Heart failure—what the hell do you think?"

"Voodoo, probably. What I think doesn't make a damn—but it sure seems to me somebody around here'd wonder why a guy in his early forties'd suddenly drop dead just two weeks after his girlfriend is clubbed to death and a deputy's poisoned."

"He didn't just drop dead—he'd been poorly for two weeks or more—"

"And everything's a Goddamned coincidence, huh?"

"I ain't got one blamed solid piece of evidence that says different. You gimme one, Carl. Just one."

"No autopsy—no search warrant—that's it?"

"That's right. Besides, Gus is already on his way to Aquatown. He's gonna be cremated."

I told Orrie he wasn't bright and put it in terms that made his anonymous note-writer sound downright flattering but I might as well have saved my breath because his jelly brain was so set in a mold that he didn't listen to a word.

Finally I charged out in a huff and made the mistake of going back to the hotel.

"Well," said Ma as I entered the door, "you're just on time—I want to transplant an elm and you can help."

She was letting me know she appreciated the fact I was clear of Flory's murder. She always had something for me to help her with when she was happy. Of course she also had something for me to do if she was unhappy but her attitude was different then. When she was mad, I was doing as she told me—when she was happy, I was helping. Besides, transplanting a tree was a happy job—she put me to something like removing varnish from an apartment floor when she was mad.

"I guess you heard about Gus," I said as we headed out back.

"Wasn't that a shame? Poor Claire—to have the family name dragged through the mud like that. Lord knows I understand what it is to be disgraced by those near and dear—"

I moved her tree, watered it till it damned near drowned

130

and got through supper with almost no more references to my disreputable past and unpromising future but once I was away from the table I headed for Boswell's, planning to wash out all the forgiveness.

We slugged the jug about an hour and a half and I suppose that's what did it. I'd been playing the sober son for longer than agreed with me and the frustrations were too much. I went over everything about the murder with Boswell who, as usual, listened patiently. He wasn't all that excited about a solution now that I wasn't in any danger but he allowed there was reason enough for me to stay involved since it had all made me shy about drinking strange booze.

"You told me," he said, "that Orrie didn't figure Nate'd hide his loot at home—maybe he's right—if he meant Loden. But what about right here in Corden? Why wouldn't he hide stuff at his ma's place?"

I thought that over and shook my head. "Not even Nate'd hide stolen stuff at his ma's."

"I dunno—you sure you don't just figure that because you don't wanna go poking around Jenny's house?"

"Look—it wouldn't be there because he couldn't bring it in without her seeing. A shotgun's not a thing you can hide in a watch pocket."

"He wouldn't have no trouble if he brought it home while she was at work."

"You sure think of everything," I told him. "Why can't you get senile and silent like an old man should?"

"Mostly I do. But now and again I slip back."

I stood up. "Fix me a flask, eh?"

"Why?"

"Because we're old buddies and I asked."

"You gonna do something foolish again?"

"I'm gonna check his place out."

"How? You just gonna drive to Loden, park in front and go in? You know where he lives, even?"

"Sure—in Loden. You gonna fix me that pint?"

He flapped his hands, grunted to his feet and got me the pint. I slapped him on the shoulder, slipped the curved bottle into my hip pocket and left.

Following a hunch I walked straight from Boswell's over to Gilbertson's Pool Hall and there was Nate. Right away I felt sure I had things figured right. Because if everything was all squared away, why was Nate still hanging around town? Was he waiting for a payoff he hadn't got, or maybe living on blackmail?

I offered to play him a game and he said no almost politely.

"I'll spot you three balls."

He made an impractical suggestion about where I could shove them, and dropped a nine ball in the side pocket with a tricky bank shot.

"You decide to retire young?" I asked.

"Just taking a little vacation," he said. He missed the ten ball.

"Come home to take care of your ma, huh?"

He kept his eye on the table, squinting a little against the smoke that drifted up from the cigarette dangling from the corner of his mouth. He pretended he was too interested in his opponent's shot to catch my question. I repeated it.

"Whatever you like, Wilcox," said Nate.

"You must get along great with old Jack Wortle—he lets you take off any old time, eh?"

"He likes me okay."

"I bet you stay right at his place, like a son, right?"

"Hell no—I got my own room at the hotel."

"Is that a fact? Got a big bed all to yourself and a lock on the door and a drawer full of spicy pulps, I bet."

"I never had to read about it."

"Come on, don't tell me you bring gals in—"

"All right, I won't tell you."

By then I had what I wanted and I left.

It took about thirty minutes to reach Loden in my truck. I parked down the street a block from the hotel and looked it over. It was a two-story building, a lot like the Wilcox Hotel only not so sprawled out and with a little fancier front. You had to go up three steps to enter the lobby and there was no screen door, just a big wooden job with thick glass in the top half and heavy paneling below. I guessed the place had maybe twenty rooms.

It was a little after ten when I walked through the front door and spotted a mean and sleepy-looking character behind the register. He gave me a sour look as I approached and my grin brought no response at all.

"I'm looking for Nate Larson," I said.

"He ain't here."

"No? He told me he was living here not three weeks ago—"

"Three weeks ago he was. Now he ain't."

"You mean when he's in town he stays at this hotel but right now he's not in town?"

"You got it all doped out, feller."

I frowned and stared around the lobby suspiciously.

"I gotta find him."

"Why?"

I scowled at him and he stared back with slate-blue eyes under bushy brows. He could have hired out as a house haunt with no touching up. His nose hooked hard enough to make the tip almost touch his upper lip, his jaw was sharp as a chisel.

"He owes me money—promised to pay. He staying in room fourteen?"

"What difference does it make? He ain't here."

"He told me he had room fourteen. Said it was really thirteen but hotels never give thirteen to any room—is that right?"

Old hooknose gave me a grin I could have done without—he looked better scowling because that didn't show his teeth. He seemed to be waking up enough to entertain himself a little.

"That's right," he said.

"That he stays in fourteen?"

"No. That we ain't got any thirteen. If he was in fourteen he'd be in thirteen but he ain't in neither."

"Well, when he is in, which is he in?"

"He stays in twenty. That's way in the back."

"Oh," I said, and looked toward the stairway off to my right.

"No," he said, "you can't go up. He ain't there and I don't allow non-guests upstairs anyway."

"That's smart," I admitted. "Old Nate give you any trouble on that score?"

"He don't bring strangers in."

"Just folks you know, huh?"

"Nobody. We don't allow no hanky-panky in this hotel—this here's a respectable place."

"I can see that. You got any notion where Nate is?"

"Don't know, don't care."

I gave him up and went out. In case he watched, I strolled down the street away from the hotel and went into the restaurant about half a block away. A gray-haired lady told me they were closing so I went back out and rubbernecked up and down the street. The place was dead as a ghost-town cemetery and nowhere near as pretty. I walked back past the hotel a couple blocks, circled back to the building's rear and looked it over. A fire escape with narrow wooden steps ran down from a stingy platform outside the last window facing west. The yard was darker than a witch's left teat and I stood for a long while, waiting for my eyes to adjust and stalling before I walked over to the steps and tested them. They were fairly new and didn't creak much.

I took a small shot from the hip flask and thought about a cigarette but decided against it. If Nate kept room twenty I figured it was right near the fire escape and ought to be easy to come by. Chances were good that the window wasn't locked—we never locked anything at the Wilcox Hotel—not even the safe—but it bothered me that there was no light by the fire escape. Handy as the darkness was for me, there was something wrong about it.

I left the steps, walked to the northeast corner, then to the southwest and gave a slow look around. Nothing was doing. I went back and started up the steps. One creaked about halfway up but wasn't noticeable and I kept going. Wind rustled the leaves of an elm in the south corner of the back lot and crickets were going at it like a million mad fiddlers. I pressed my head against the wall and heard nothing.

"What the hell," I thought, and reached for the window. The screen blocked me. I checked its edges and found no wing nuts so it meant the blamed thing was hung from the top and hooked on the inside bottom. I took out my penknife and pried a little but there was no give. I took another slug from the hip flask, screwed the top on, shoved it back in my pocket, and gently shoved my penknife through the screen. It was old stuff but a long ways from shot and it raised hell with my blade. I made an inverted T opening in a second, pushed through and unlatched the hook.

Naturally the damned screen didn't just swing open. Some bastard had painted the sill since spring and the screen was firmly stuck.

I took a good hold where I'd made the opening and the screen cut my palm. What I said, if it'd been out loud, would've blistered the paint. I jerked experimentally, then some harder and crack! The screen gave way and popped open.

I was still sitting crouched like a constipated cat, waiting for the echoes to fade, when a light came on and I found myself staring into a bedroom at a gray-haired old lady who sat up, holding a sheet against her chin, staring at me in horror.

"Sorry, lady," I said politely, "wrong room."

A half-second later I was down the steps and pegging for the truck. I expected a scream or yells or even shots but there wasn't a blessed sound in my wake.

As a precaution I headed south out of town and then worked my way back east and on home.

Nobody chased me.

CHAPTER
18

I was watering the transplanted elm the next afternoon when Orrie came around.

"So you got a snootful again last night," he said, scowling.

"So?"

"And you just couldn't keep from going over to Loden and checking around the hotel where Nate stayed, eh?"

"Who—me?"

"I got a call from the town cop. He says a fella with sneaky eyes was in the hotel asking about Nate Larson and a little later, this sneaky-eyed fella tried to rape an old lady."

"Now that's bullshit—you don't believe it—do you?"

"Well," said Orrie, "you owe old man Clinton for a new screen."

"A whole screen? Hell, he could repair it easy—the damned thing's all rotten—"

"He wants the whole screen. He's willing to put it in himself."

"Goddamnit, this is extortion."

"Uh-huh—you want a trial?"

"Hell no—I'll pay—but I don't admit a damned thing and I think the ethics of the law in South Dakota are pretty damned shoddy."

He said my tongue was still thick with last night's booze and took my money.

"If you'd just got the search warrant, I wouldn't've had to go through all that," I said.

"You wouldn't even if I had just checked things out." He was all of a sudden in a painfully good mood and grinned at me.

"What the hell's that mean?"

"I mean Nate didn't keep the room. It ain't permanent—you know? You was in the right place but old lady Bermeister's been staying there a week."

I just about gave up the detecting business on the spot. I doubt I've ever been more disgusted. And then I thought of something.

"It's in his car," I said.

"Yeah—I thought of that."

"You don't need a search warrant to look in his car, do you?"

"Could be—I ain't real sure. But maybe we could work it out a little sneakier than that. What I mean is, if it ain't there and he really did swipe that stuff, he'll be all warned and we maybe won't ever find anything."

"Okay—tonight, if he stays at Jenny's, I'll let the air out of his tire and you just arrange to come by early in the morning, notice it, and stop to help."

"I don't think that'd work too good. Never know when Nate might get up—or if he'll stay at Jenny's. Maybe it'd be better if you just slip down the alley to where his Buick's parked right now and let the air out while he's playing pool. Then I can tell him about the flat and we'll see if he's willing to go open that trunk with me by."

It worked slick. Nobody was in sight and I unscrewed the valve and inhaled the rubbery stink as the tire went flat. I tightened it back and strolled around the block past the front of Gilbertson's. Orrie was parked across the street watching and a few minutes later he waddled back of the pool hall and in through the rear door. I went back to the hotel, climbed upstairs and looked out from room nine. It gave me a middling-fair view of the alley and Nate's car. Pretty soon Nate came out with Orrie. He didn't seem too mad but of course I couldn't hear him and in no time he'd opened the trunk and was hauling out tools. Orrie stood right at his elbow and even helped him take the spare out. I knew then there wasn't going to be any shotgun or pistol in the trunk, let alone a can of rat poison.

I decided to go over to Boswell's and spend the night boozing. The hell with it.

By midnight I was feeling no pain and the whole business of the Loden trip seemed funnier than hell. Boswell pretended he was horrified but couldn't keep from grinning at the description of the old lady's face when she spotted me outside her window.

He was still grinning as Orrie's tin Lizzie pulled up in front of the shack and Orrie climbed down to stare at us disapprovingly.

"Now what?" I asked.

"Ever since you come back to town," he growled, "we've had a Goddamned crime wave."

Boswell offered him a drink and at first he shook his head but then thought better of it and took the bottle. After a healthy swig he wiped his mouth, handed the bottle back and hunkered down. We were sitting on chairs set against the shack wall.

"Jeff Catton's wife shot him tonight."

"Shot Jeff?"

"Uh-huh."

"Jesus—she found out he's been seeing Lil?"

"I guess so. Of course she claims it was an accident—so does he."

"You mean he's not dead?"

"Of course he's not dead, for Christ's sake, he couldn't have called it an accident if she'd killed him, could he?"

"After Gus's confession, nothing'd surprise me."

"She shot him in the leg. The right one. I think she was aiming at the family jewels. Scared the shit out of him I can tell you—"

"Small wonder."

"Yeah—but what's interesting is what she used to shoot 'im with. It's the pistol stolen from the hardware store in Aquatown."

"Where'd she get it?"

He grunted, stood up and arched his back. "Gettin' too old to hunker, damnit. Where'd she get it? From Jeff's top drawer. It's his—he says. I asked where he got it and he said he found it in the men's room at Gilbertson's."

"You believe that?"

"Sure, just like I believe in the tooth fairy—but that's all I can get out of him."

"What'd you do?"

"I got his wife's okay to search the house and me and Willie went over the whole damned place, top to bottom. No shotgun, no other stolen stuff I could see. Not a single, contrary Goddamned thing. But Jeff was in Aquatown the night of the robbery. Him and Jimmy Quint. They spent the night in town—Jeff wants me to think it was in a whorehouse—Big Nose Ruth's—he didn't say so in front of his wife but that's the address he gave me—where her place is, I mean."

"How'd you know where Big Nose Ruth's place is?"

"I'm a cop. Cops are supposed to know things like that."

"How'd you like her stock?"

"I never bought any—I'm not as horny as you—or as careless—"

"You really think Jeff'd rob a place?"

"Well, he sure as hell didn't find that gun in Gilbertson's."

When Orrie left us I corked the jug, set it beside Boswell and told him I'd see him around.

"Where you going?"

"Think I'll get laid."

"You figure Lil sold the gun to Jeff?"

"Could be."

"I never heard of Lil doing any business she couldn't manage on her back."

"Lil does business in all positions, Bos. You wouldn't believe how many she knows. *I* don't believe and I've been through all of 'em."

Lil was sitting on her front porch when I ambled up the walk a little after midnight. I sat down on the stoop and said good evening.

"I'm not working tonight," she said.

"I didn't think it was ever work for you."

"Well," she said, frowning, "that shows how much you know."

"I guess you wouldn't mind talking some?"

"I ain't eager."

"I guess you heard about Jeff?"

"You bet your life—I heard *all* about it. I don't want to hear any more."

"What about the gun?"

She looked at me warily. "What gun?"

"The one his wife shot him with. A nice little blue pistol somebody stole this month from a hardware store in Aquatown. You didn't hear about that?"

She looked away. "All I heard was she shot him. Over me. I bet it wasn't over me at all. She was mad 'cause he

141

never wanted any at home and he didn't just come here, I'll tell you that. It's not my fault."

"I don't know, Lil, you make a lot of wives seem like pretty thin beer."

"It didn't take me to make her seem like that."

I rolled two cigarettes, lit them, passed one up and leaned my elbow on the porch floor.

"Orrie thinks Jeff robbed that hardware store."

"That's stupid."

"You think he'd be smart if he believed Jeff's claim he found it in Gilbertson's can?"

"Jeff wouldn't steal anything—at least he wouldn't bust into a place to do it."

I thought that was a reasonably shrewd notion. Nine out of ten guys won't break in, but damned near that many will lift anything left loose if it's tempting enough.

"Jeff's gonna have a hell of a time making anybody believe that. He's gonna need help, Lil."

"You make that sound like it's supposed to come from me."

"That's the idea. Was it a deal straight between Nate and Jeff, or was it through you?"

"I never touched the thing—I never stole nothing or sold what anybody else stole—what I sell is all mine, by God."

"You just borrow other women's men now and again, huh?"

"They come to me—I don't go out after them."

I grinned at her. "Did Nate really bring you flowers?"

She started to turn red with anger, then settled back and glared at me. "Why's that so damned hard to believe?"

"It's not hard to believe a guy'd want to give you flowers. I just don't figure Nate's smart enough to think of it or big enough to do it."

"Yeah," she sighed, "you're right."

"It was Nate that sold the gun to Jeff—right?"

"I suppose so. They were talking in the kitchen—I didn't pay that much attention."

"Did you see the gun?"

"Yeah, sure."

"Nate say where he got it?"

"Said his daddy left it to him. He went on about how he hated to sell it but needed the money."

"He offer to sell his old man's shotgun too?"

"Yeah—how'd you know that?"

"Did Jeff buy it?"

"Not the shotgun—said he already had one."

"Did you see the shotgun?"

"Naw—Nate didn't carry that in—I wouldn't have stood for that."

"Did he go out to his car to get the gun you saw?"

"No. He had it in his pocket."

So he probably still had the shotgun. I was just as happy to hear he'd tried to sell it. That suggested he wasn't saving it for me. On the other hand that might beat worrying about whether my booze was going to be poisoned.

I looked up at Lil who was rocking back and forth in her chair. She was pulling such a long face it was almost laughable.

"When I talked to you before, Lil, you said Nate didn't talk to the guys. Now you say he sold a gun to Jeff. Which is true?"

"What I just told you."

"Why'd you lie before?"

"I don't know. I do it a lot—aren't whores supposed to?"

"You're not a whore, Lil—you just like loving. Were you leveling when you said Nate was drunk?"

"Honest to God. He was *really* drunk—ask Jeff."

"If Jeff won't admit where he got that gun, he's going to prison."

"Oh, God," she wailed, "I wish I could talk to him—"

"How about I take a message?"

Her eyes opened wide and she leaned toward me. "Would you, Carl?"

"Sure."

She dropped her cigarette, stepped on it and sat back.

"Tell him I'll say who sold him the gun if he says the word."

"Is that all?"

"Tell 'im I'm sorry about what happened—only don't say it where his wife can hear—okay?"

"Not likely."

"You really are nice, Carl," she said, smiling.

"Nice enough to go upstairs with?"

"Not tonight. It wouldn't seem right, you know?"

"Maybe it'd take your mind off your worries."

"It might for a little while—then I'd only feel worse. I don't want to get my mind off too soon. It wouldn't seem right if it was that easy."

It turned cool during the night and Sunday morning the wind rose, bringing dust off the prairie, sifting it through door and window cracks and filtering the sun until it was a bright disc, red and sore, like a mortified eye.

After lunch I asked the old man if he'd loan me his car for a few hours.

"What's wrong with your truck?"

"It's near out of gas and it uses more than the Dodge."

"But the gas in the Dodge is mine."

"Okay—loan me enough cash to buy gas for the truck."

He thought that over and decided I could borrow the car. The hardest thing in the world for Elihu to do was reach in his back pocket, remove the wallet and take money out.

It was near two o'clock in the afternoon when I got to the hospital. Jeff was sitting up in bed, playing cribbage with a gawky geezer in a maroon bathrobe. Jeff lost and the old geezer tottered off, happy as a fresh-laid sailor.

I asked Jeff how he felt and we exchanged the usual before getting to the point.

"Lil told me where you got the gun. She says she'll tell Orrie if you give the word."

"Carl, I don't want Bess to know where that gun come from."

"I don't see what difference it'd make—you think she'll use an ax the next time?"

"I don't want her to know."

"You're ready to go to prison?"

"It won't come to that."

"Don't bet your ass on it. I'm gonna give you a little tip, Jeff, it's free but good as gold—the fact that you know you're just about the greatest guy in the world won't keep you out of the pen a second. I thought so once—figured everybody knew old Carl was a great fella—wouldn't harm anybody for anything—but nobody's got the same opinion of us we've got—except a few mothers—and they'll slap you in the keep quick's a cat can lick her ass and with no more thought."

He made a face so hurt I thought for a second he was going to bawl, then he sighed and asked if I thought Orrie would keep it to himself if Lil spilled.

"He might if he can—but don't plan on it. Goddamnit, Bess knows you been up there—that's why she shot you—so what the hell difference does more about it make?"

"You don't know women much, Carl. It's just gonna be more fussin' and ranting—"

"Listen—fussin' and ranting beat prison all to hell. Let me tell you about what kind of a zoo it is—"

Before long he waved his hands at me and said, "Okay—tell her to unload on Orrie. Goddamn, I'd love to brain Nate—"

• • •

I wheeled back to Corden, went up to Lil's and brought her down to see Orrie. He asked a lot of questions, made out a statement and had her sign it.

"Your word ain't worth much," he told her, "but for Jeff it might do. And now you'd better go out of business for a while. Take a trip or hide your tail. If you go to carrying on like you been, I'll lock you up."

Lil's sloe eyes narrowed and her face turned red. I was blamed glad she'd already signed the statement but for a second thought she'd snatch it up and rip it apart. When I made a little movement toward her she gave me a dirty look and tightened her lips.

"You got that?" pushed Orrie.

"For Christ's sake," I said, "of course she's got it—get off her back."

"I just want to be sure she stays off hers—I got more trouble than I need with this murder thing and I'll put it to you plain—I could make a lot of folks think I was great if I threw her ass in the cell. I don't want she should forget that."

I stood up. "Come on, Lil, I'll drive you home."

"Let her walk," said Orrie. "It ain't gonna help things if you two start getting thick—"

I told him to shove that and Lil jerked her head at him as she sailed out ahead of me but once she was in the car she slumped down in the seat and leaned against the far door as we drove up the hill.

"Don't worry," I told her, "this'll pass over and everything will be fine."

"Everything'll stink," she said hoarsely. "Everything always stinks."

"No. It's always up and down—never the same. You'll **bounce—I know you, Lil.**"

"Like hell you do."

There's no sense in arguing with a woman in a mood like that so I shut up. When we pulled up in front of her place she straightened up slowly, stared at the house for several seconds and then turned to give me a long, slow look.

"Would you want to marry me?" she demanded.

"Lil—I'm not a marrying man."

"Damned right—not where Lil's concerned. And you're nothing but a bum. So what'll happen? I'll get too old to give anybody a good time and be left alone in this damned funeral parlor Pa left me. I can't sell it—who'd buy a whorehouse in Corden? I can't go away 'cause I'd have no place to live, so what the hell will I do?"

"Lil, you're a hell of a ways from old and it doesn't take any time to change. Listen—how about I take you to a dance in Aquatown, or out to Harper's Lake sometime. You could meet some different guys and—"

"They'd all be married—or they'd have heard about me. It'd stink."

"Hell, Lil, everybody knows a good whore makes a good wife—you'd find a guy if that's what you wanted. But you got to really want—you can't just sit on your can up here and wait for Prince Charming."

"I never read any fairy story where the girl went out and found the guy."

"That's what makes a fairy story a fairy story—they're not real."

"They're *that* real—the guys come to the girls."

She didn't really want to be comforted—she was suffering and needed it and so I told her I'd see her soon and she said sure and went up to her big empty house.

Orrie didn't bitch at me when I went back to City Hall and we sat there awhile not talking about Lil.

"Aren't you gonna pick up Nate?" I asked.

He nodded.

"You don't seem to be in any thundering rush."

"Think a little about what we got so far," he said. "We got evidence that Nate maybe robbed that store in Aquatown and sold a stolen gun in Corden. We got Jeff's word that the gun came from Nate. We got nothing more than that. You think Nate killed Flory and tried to poison you—but we got nothing solid to back that—"

"We got Lil to witness the gun sale—"

"A whore's testimony ain't worth a fart in a whirlwind, Carl. No, you can't sell a jury on anything she says—nor a judge. In this case we got Nate's word against Jeff's."

"Maybe, if Nate hears they've told on him, he'll admit the whole thing."

"Nate wouldn't admit to being born 'less he gave it a day's thought and figured it'd pay. If we was dealing with a fella like Gus, I'd say, sure, he'd open like a wet envelope once you spotted him—but Nate's another case. And don't plan on finding that shotgun or the rat poison—he's ditched 'em both, long ago."

"Unless he was saving one or both for another killing."

"Why'd he kill again? He's got the job done."

"Maybe a man gets to liking it. I've heard of guys doing that."

He grunted, got to his feet and put on his hat.

"I hate like hell doing this to Jenny," he said. "It might scare off her fiancé."

"If it does, he's no Goddamned good and she'll be better off knowing it."

"Yeah—you'd think that. You want to come along?"

I did and I didn't but I said yes and went. It seemed like it'd be too chicken to set things up and then hide out while everything happened.

Jenny's was only a walk away but Orrie figured official

visits had to be made by car and we rode over in his tin
Lizzie, parked in the drive and looked around. The Buick
wasn't in sight and we hadn't seen it on Main Street so
Orrie sat a few seconds, puzzling over that before he
sighed, opened the door and climbed out. I trailed him to
the kitchen door where Jenny met us.

"Nate around?" asked Orrie.

Jenny looked through the screen at me. It veiled her face
but even so she looked some drained—like there'd been
no sleep and lots of worry.

"No, why?"

"Just want to talk with him. Got any notion where he'd
be?"

"No. He left while I was at church."

"Where you think he might go, Jenny?"

"I haven't the foggiest notion. What do you want to talk
to him about?"

"A little problem. Maybe you could help me out—did
your husband ever own a pistol?"

"No."

"You sure of that?"

"Yes. Why is Carl Wilcox with you when you come to
ask Nate questions?"

"Well, it's sort of complicated, Jenny—he's been helping
me a little on a case—"

"He thinks Nate killed Flory—but you've already got
Gus's confession—so now what do you want?"

She talked low but her voice was edgy and trembling.

"This don't *have* to have anything to do with Flory. This
is about a shooting last night—"

"You mean Bess—who shot that tomcat husband of
hers?"

"That's right. Jeff claims he bought the gun off Nate—
that Nate says it was his pa's."

"Well," said Jenny, brushing hair from her forehead,

"maybe he did. I don't know everything Joe owned. He had lots of strange things and he was close with Nate—I wouldn't necessarily know—"

"Fine, fine," said Orrie soothingly. "Okay, if Nate shows up, you ask him to stop by City Hall and see me. I'd appreciate that—and don't you worry, Jenny."

Back in his office I asked Orrie if there was more than one whorehouse in Aquatown.

"Yeah—how many you need, for Christ's sake?"

"I was thinking of Nate—Lil's out of business—he's got money—so where's he getting it?"

"So you want to go checking out whorehouses on Sunday?"

"You going to deputize me?"

"Not for Aquatown—no jurisdiction."

"I knew I could depend on you."

CHAPTER
19

On Monday morning, two weeks after Flory's death, I ate breakfast, did a few chores and then slipped out of the hotel and made a tour of town looking for Nate's Buick. Not finding it, I climbed into my truck and headed for Aquatown.

The whole countryside was like a dusty frying pan sitting in an oven at broil. I could spot car trails a mile off—their yellow dust rolled over twenty feet high, thick as oil smoke which hung steady, twisting slow long after the cars moved out of sight.

I drove steady at forty-five, avoiding loose gravel beside the ditch, and recalled my last talk with Orrie. He'd said I had no business hunting up Nate—if I found him I'd only get myself in a jam when he turned ornery—which he'd sure as hell do at the sight of me.

I had talked Orrie into putting out a pick-up order on Nate and said I'd just locate him, report to the local cops where he was and we'd be in business. If he'd agree to deputize me, I could even bring Nate back myself.

"You want Jenny to know you dragged her boy back?" he asked.

I said forget it—I'd just turn him in to the local cops and come back alone. So he put out the order and I left.

Of course it didn't turn out that simple.

I drove past Big Nose Ruth's and found no Buick. I took a

swing past every hotel in town and again came up blank. For a little while I drove up and down streets where it seemed most likely there'd be boardinghouses or sporting houses but still came up dry.

Aquatown's only got about twelve thousand people so it's not too hard to cover and it wasn't surprising that as I passed a used-car lot I spotted the big Buick. I went in and chinned with a young salesman for a while. He was friendly as a spaniel pup and about as bright. Any salesman with a day's experience would have known I wasn't going to buy anything but he talked for the joy of it and details of making a living didn't fuss him any. Eventually I learned that a lean, smiley kid had traded the Buick in on a Graham Paige.

"How come?" I asked.

"I kind of wondered myself," said the kid. "I mean, they're the same year and one's about as big as the other but this fella said he wanted a change and sure as heck I wasn't going to argue. Paid cash on the difference and took off. Seemed a nice enough guy but he wasn't much for talking and he never gave me a straight answer to a question. I'm not nosy—just friendly—like to jaw with customers—that's why I'm a salesman. Grandma always said I had the gift of gab—said I'd more than likely make a good lawyer but I never wanted any of that—dealing with criminal types and stuff—why'd anybody want to do that?"

I couldn't think of one good reason that would impress him but he wasn't waiting for an answer so he never missed it.

The Graham Paige showed up parked on a side street near the Bridge Hotel. It wasn't the classiest part of town, it looked like the wrong side of the tracks on skid row. I went up a two-step rise to the entrance which was on the corner and looked over a lobby about half again as big as the Wilcox Hotel's but there were no fans, canaries or rocking chairs in sight. A dying sofa sagged against the wall on my right, two overstuffed chairs leaned toward each other on my left and a gray, bun-haired woman with a button nose and a mouth too small to suck a straw sat in a swivel chair beside the registration counter. She squinted as I came in and walked toward her.

She took a stab at a smile and got the mouth hole almost half an inch wide.

"Hi," I said, "I'm looking for a fella named Nate Larson—kind of a thin fella, taller than me, real smiley."

The tiny mouth managed a droop and admitted that Mr. Larson had a room. I asked was he in. She wasn't sure—I could go look if I liked. He had number thirty-one.

I liked. The stairway was covered with rubber runners and creaked discreetly at every step. At the top I found two long corridors running north and west and a short corridor to my left, running south. Small letters on the near wall told me rooms twenty to thirty-six were along the north corridor and I walked silently over a threadbare carpet under occasional, grimy-glassed skylights. At the Wilcox Hotel, empty-room doors were always left open—Ma claimed it gave the place a friendlier feel, and I could see what she meant. The closed doors seemed hostile.

Number thirty-one was on my right and I stopped beside it and listened for a second but heard nothing. I knocked. Nothing happened. I knocked again, a little harder and waited, listening. Some guy in the west wing blew his nose with a honk that'd do justice to a diesel train but that was all I heard. I tried the door which opened without a sound. Green shades, drawn past the open windowsills, flapped inward as the door opened and made me jerk back before I realized it was only a draft. The windows flanked a double bed with a headboard pushed against the wall. An open suitcase gaped at me from a chair at the foot of the bed and a shirt drooped from the left bedpost near me. I looked behind the door and saw nothing but wall hooks and striped wallpaper with a gaping seam. For a second I stood, looking around at the sparse furniture and the worn carpet. The bedspread was wrinkled on the left but the pillows were still puffed and tight under the bedroll.

There was no closet and hiding anything in a big cell like that seemed hopeless but I took a peek under the bed, shifted stuff in the suitcase a little and then went over to check outside the window. I'd just pulled the right-hand shade to one side and got a glimpse of the street when I heard the door open behind me.

"You lookin' for this?" asked Nate.

I dropped the shade and turned to look down a sawed-off shotgun barrel. No—two barrels.

He looked pretty happy at the other end. I envied him. A lot of crazy ideas went through my head—like would it rattle him if I jerked the shade so it went up with a clatter—but I decided all that'd do was get me blown through the window.

"I saw you down there, rubbernecking around. In case you're wondering, this thing's loaded. It's only birdshot, though. No range at all. If you can get far enough it might not hardly hurt at all. I know you're fast—you wanna make a run for it?"

I wasn't ready to risk even talking. I shook my head.

He walked crabwise over to the bureau and without taking his eyes or the gun muzzles from me, tried to open the top drawer with his left hand. The right stayed firm on the shotgun grip and his finger was over the trigger. The drawer, a full-length type with two handles, jammed when he pulled on just one. He yanked it impatiently and sweat popped out on my head. I knew how easy it would be to jerk the trigger while he was struggling with the other hand. After some jiggling he got the drawer open, lifted a pint hip flask and tossed it on the bed.

"Stick that in your pocket," he said. "You and me are going to take a little walk."

I was still short on bright chatter and I picked up the flask as ordered. He moved back to the door, still keeping the shotgun level with my middle which felt naked and prickly.

He opened the door, stuck his head out, looked both ways and backed straight into the hall. When he jerked his head at me I followed, slow and easy. He kept me in sight, moved a step to the south and waved me into the north corridor.

"The woman downstairs knows I came up looking for you," I said. "So does Orrie."

He grinned wider than ever. "That's gonna help you a hell of a lot. Go on down the hall to the end and open the window."

I walked slowly, partly to keep him calm and partly hoping someone would open one of those hostile doors. Nobody did.

The window opened easy and I looked out on a fire escape that ran down to a vacant alley. There was a railing about three feet high on each side of a little platform over the ladder.

Walking down the long hall had given me time to cool some and I'd made up my mind by the time I reached the window that if I ever let him get me to the ground I was a dead man so it was a matter of figuring what crazy move would give me the best chance. I decided I'd slam the window down when he started through.

"Go headfirst," he told me, "and don't turn around. Make one move and your ass'll be mash."

So much for slamming the window.

I went through the opening, jumping to the top of the platform railing, grabbed the roof overhang, jerked up my knees and went over in one motion that landed me face-down on the flat roof.

Nate was so surprised to see me disappear he didn't take time to brace for the shot and it knocked him flat on his ass when he jerked the trigger and let go with both barrels. I heard the clatter of his fall after the shot.

Leaping to my feet I charged across the tarred roof like a cat with a kerosened ass, dodged a chimney and ran in a line with that to the roof's edge overlooking the street faced by Nate's room. It would have been lovely if there'd been a balcony all around, but there was nothing but sidewalk two floors down. I wasn't scared enough to risk it. I ran back to the chimney, peeked around and ducked back, sure that Nate would be sighting over the roof edge. He wasn't. For several seconds I squatted behind the chimney, feeling the sun hot on my back and smelling the blistered tar that covered the roof under a layer of sand. I listened and heard only sparrows chattering somewhere out of sight.

After a few more seconds I began looking for a trapdoor that'd let me back inside. The one I found didn't tempt me—it must have been within a few yards of Nate's room—which he may have returned to. Not being too eager to eyeball the shotgun again, I set off in a low crouch and soon reached the wing that ran north, which gave me a view of the west-wing fire escape. There was no sign of Nate. I went to the north edge of the roof and looked down on a sloping roof, thought about one second, swung over, let myself dangle, pushed out just a hint and dropped.

I landed with knees bent, back arched, feet perfectly together—everything right—only the damned roof collapsed like a raspberry box. Probably I was lucky—if it hadn't caved under me I'd have spilled backwards on the sloping roof and landed on my face in the rear drive. I didn't go through the roof—it just gave completely and I landed on my back and rolled like a beach ball into the gravel. Without losing momentum I came to my feet and took off at a dead run.

My legs are a hell of a lot too bowed for competitive racing but when inspired they work better than your run-of-the-mill citizen can match and I was out of sight and reach in a few seconds.

It took about five minutes to find a telephone and feed in money for a long-distance call to Orrie.

I told him what had happened and while talking suddenly remembered the flask on my hip. A quick check told me it was okay—which was pretty miraculous considering my recent carryings-on.

Orrie wanted me to go report my experiences to the local cops and I nixed that. "They'll try to make me pay for that damned shed roof and I'm not gonna."

He said I was being ridiculous, they'd understand and I told him no cop, including him, understands an ex-con and the hell with it—I was coming back. All he had to do was tell the cops where to find Nate. He started fussing as the operator came on to say I had to make another deposit and I hung up.

As I climbed down from the truck cab about forty minutes later, Orrie came bustling around the west corner of City Hall. His face was red with excitement and heat and I told him he'd ought to sit down and take it easy before he had a tizzy fit.

"I've talked with Talbot," he said, "that's the chief in Aquatown—he says Nate took off—left his suitcase in the room and grabbed his car and hauled ass. Didn't pay his bill."

"Well, you got him cold on one violation now, huh? Want to check out this pint he gave me?"

"You figure it's like what he gave Torky?"

"Careful—you got no evidence—remember?"

"If this thing's poisoned, I got plenty evidence, by God."

We went over to Doc's together and after some fiddling around Doc told us it was sure enough loaded with strychnine. Orrie went and called Aquatown to say they didn't just want Nate for questioning—they figured he was sure enough a killer. A cop killer, at that.

After Orrie hung up we sat in his office and I was grinning because it was fine to be right and even better to be alive.

"Well," said Orrie, "I guess I better go tell Jenny."

All the grin and good was gone like that. I felt sick.

Orrie watched me.

"I gotta tell her," he said. "If he comes back to her place, she's gotta know."

"I'll tell her," I said.

He took a deep breath, let it out slow and looked out the window at Main Street's heat waves.

"You think it'd come easier from you?"

"Maybe not." It disgusted me that I hoped he'd talk me out of it and it disgusted me that he looked like a toad sitting there with his damned gun and billy club and big belly. "Maybe yes. Anyway, I'll do it."

"That's real fine, Carl, I'd surely appreciate it."

I knew Jenny was at work and it wasn't the right place to tell her anything personal so I strolled out to the house. In a town like Corden a stranger can drive through on a normal afternoon and think there's not half a dozen people alive in the place. I walked three blocks without seeing anybody but Stu Craven, a retired shoe-store owner, digging in a flower patch in front of his house. While walking, I thought about Nate and what he might do.

As far as I knew, he'd never been much further from home than Aquatown and Loden—maybe to the Cities once. I suspected if he was on the run he'd go for the Cities or California. They were the only alternatives for South Dakota fugitives—whether they were running from wives, families or the law they only knew the two directions. On the other hand, Nate was cuter than average, and a hell of a lot more vindictive. It was just possible he'd feel a need to kiss me good-bye personally before he left the state for good. I don't ordinarily figure myself that important to other people but this was a special deal. And it was also possible, I figured, that Nate might think he needed a final stake from Claire.

There was a notion that stuck with me. I decided once I'd talked to Jenny, I'd mosey around to the Gardner place and maybe spend a share of the night keeping an eye on things.

I came down on Jenny's place from the west hill, walking slow and looking around sharp. There were only two houses along the upper half of the block, one on each corner, and between them was a half filled-in basement where Clanton's place had burned down several years before. Everything was grown up in weeds, bushes and grass. There was no alley. Wild plums, chokecherry trees and a few crab apple trees drew kids in August and September and once in a while the Johnson clan played cowboy around the abandoned basement but that day nobody was in sight. I stood among the chokecherry trees and looked down at Jenny's barn and the white clapboard house half a rod beyond. The Johnson dog, a friendly-faced brown and white mutt, came around the house corner at a side-angle trot and halted when he spotted me. Then his tail started going and he dropped his head and came trotting up to dance around and get his head scratched.

I went through the ritual with him and then drifted down closer to the barn, looked inside and found the car stall empty. I was about to head down toward the house when the mutt halted, lifted his left forepaw and looked toward the barn loft. The hair on the back of my neck felt prickly but I managed to act as if I hadn't noticed anything and walked down toward the house. After a second the mutt followed me. I was glad he wasn't a barker.

Of course it didn't have to be Nate. Not too many years back I'd been in that loft myself, with Jenny, but she sure as hell wasn't up there on a Monday afternoon. It could be Danny—or a cat—or even a mouse—

"More like a rat," I told myself, and knocked on the shed door. In a couple seconds Danny showed up in the kitchen opening. His eyes looked too wide for normal.

"I bet you've been reading," I said.

"Uh—yeah."

"*Archie and Mehitabel?*"

"No—I finished that."

"What are you into now?"

"Well, I was reading in the *World Book*. Mom's not here—she's at work."

"Yeah, I figured that. How about Nate?"

"Nate? No—no, he's not here."

He said *here* with an emphasis he didn't intend and I could see a look of worry cross his face. He had to be the most honest kid I ever saw in my life.

"Seen him lately?"

"Not *real* lately."

I was tempted to ask if that meant not in the last five minutes but it seemed mean so I grinned and shrugged. "Well, it's not important. I was just out and around and thought I'd stop by. Guess I'll go meet Jenny when she leaves work and walk her home."

I couldn't catch any particular reaction to that but figured he'd be out to warn Nate by the time we came back. If possible, I didn't want Jenny to even see him—I didn't want her having to make a decision about whether she could help a fugitive.

Jenny didn't know whether to be mad or worried when she spotted me waiting outside the courthouse. She looked fresh as dew on new grass and almost as cool in a black and white dress and white shoes. At the sight of me her nose went up a little and she walked stiff.

"What I got to tell you," I said, as I joined her, "is no kidding matter and it sure as hell is no pleasure—"

She stopped to face me.

"It's about Nate."

"Yeah—come on, let's walk."

She glanced nervously at the people coming out of the building and moved on with me.

"I saw him in Aquatown a few hours ago. He had a shotgun he stole from a hardware store there. He shot it at me and he's on the run."

She almost stopped again, but after a break in stride, kept walking while she frowned at me.

"He shot at you?"

"That's right." I kept my tone calm even though I was madder than hell that she obviously didn't believe me and was only trying to figure out what I was after. I didn't figure I'd ever done anything to make her think I was that wild a liar. Of course the trouble was she didn't want to believe it about Nate so her reaction—or rejection—was automatic—it had nothing to do with me or even us.

"Where is he now?" she asked. She began to walk faster.

"Nobody knows for sure—but if he comes home, Orrie wants you to know he's wanted and he doesn't want you getting in trouble over Nate—you understand?"

"No, I don't understand at all. A mother is going to help her son if he's in trouble and nobody's going to put her in jail for that—not in Corden. There's been some mistake, that's all—" She glared at me. "What did you do to make Nate shoot at you—if he did?"

"I found his room in the hotel in Aquatown—I was looking around in it when he showed up with the shotgun and told me we were going for a walk and he started me down a fire escape only I went over the roof. So he busted loose with both barrels only he did it a little too late—"

"He was trying to scare you, that's all—"

"He did damned good at it—he damned near scared me to death."

"So you think you can send him to jail."

"Jenny—that's the shotgun stolen from the same store at the same time the poison was picked up that killed Torkelson. A witness says he bought a pistol from Nate that was stolen in the same place—"

"Nate can explain it," said Jenny, nodding as she hurried on, "I know he can."

"Sure—he always has, hasn't he?"

We were at the walk to her house by then and she stopped and looked at me. Her face was pale but her mouth was steady and her jaw firm.

"Good-bye, Carl," she said.

I watched her go up the three steps, across the porch and through the screen door. It was a routine we'd worn smooth in the past eight years—her going in mad at me, breaking off forever, but I knew this time was the last and I felt I'd ought to be miserable sad. The awful thing is that—like her—I found a substitute for misery in hate. She hated me and I hated her son.

I wanted to kill him.

CHAPTER
20

It was quite a problem.

I could wait on the hill behind the barn and trail Nate when he took off after dark—assuming I saw him. Or I could stake myself out at Claire's, waiting for him to show up there for his last payoff. But how could I know if he'd stayed in the barn while I went to meet Jenny?

The simplest thing, I figured, was to charge the barn and make Nate give up or shoot me. That way I'd either have him or prove to Jenny that he was a killer. The hitch was, if he did knock me off, Jenny'd figure it was self-defense and somehow that kind of comedy didn't tickle me any. Besides, I'd really feel like the prize ass if he'd already gone.

I walked around the block and worked back down into brush overlooking the barn. A big-mouthed jay took off, squawking. Nothing else moved. That might mean Danny had told his mother Nate was gone, or hadn't told her he was in the barn, or even that Jenny knew but figured I'd be watching and was too smart to give it away by visiting him.

It was a useless business—I wasn't about to wait in the brush until dark when it was possible Nate could slip away unseen if he hadn't already gone. If he didn't go to see Claire, I'd have no chance of tying her into the killings anyway and it was a good bet that cops would eventually pick up Nate if he took off. He wasn't smart enough, I didn't think, to be a good fugitive for long.

I hiked back to City Hall and walked in on Orrie while he was talking on the telephone. He ignored me as I sat down to wait.

He was listening so hard his knuckles were white from mashing his ear with the receiver. Every now and then his head bobbed. Finally he said okay, he'd do that, and hung up.

A wise expression came over his fat mug as he turned to me. "You got something new?" he asked.

"I think Nate's holed up in Jenny's barn," I said, and then explained what had happened.

"Uh-huh—real alert, Carl—you got a sharp eye." He stood up, put on his hat, walked to the door and grinned back at me. "The only trouble is—that phone call—it was from Chief Talbot. They picked up Nate in the city half an hour ago."

I managed to keep my chin from hitting the floor, but barely.

"Is it positive?" I asked.

"It seems pretty likely—fella fits our description to a tee—oh yeah, and one other little detail—he's got Nate's wallet. It's him all right."

"Where'd they find him?"

"Drunk in an alley."

"I'll be damned."

"Him too. Couldn't happen to a more deserving fella. Well, you keep your sharp eye on the town, eh? I'm going to pick up Nate—be back in a couple hours."

I guess I never had a hangover that left me feeling emptier than that news. It should have been great because I didn't have to worry about being bushwhacked now, but I always took pride in figuring people and I couldn't believe Danny had fooled me at the house or that Nate was the kind who'd get falling down drunk when he knew every cop in the state was looking for him.

It was well past supper time at the hotel and I knew it'd only get me a callused ear if I tried to coax Bertha into fixing me up so I drifted over to Gus's Café. The supper crowd had thinned to nothing. Rose brought me the short ribs and I ate slowly while keeping an eye out for Claire. I had a hunch her marble brow'd break out in an honest-to-humanity sweat when she heard that Nate was being picked up. It wasn't until I was on my third cup of coffee and hoping for a good belch that it dawned on me Claire wasn't around.

"Where's the queen?" I asked Rose.

"Mrs. Gardner? She left just before you came in."

"Oh—she go out to find a decent place to eat?"

"Don't be silly," she said, frowning. "It was real queer—she up and left sudden—after taking everything from the cash register but the small change."

"What happened just before that?"

"I don't know—I was out in the kitchen talking to Joel."

I put out my cigarette and turned to Dedee who was clearing a table near us.

"Did Claire get a telephone call?" I asked her.

She looked frightened, but nodded. I got up and walked slowly over beside her. "Dedee, this is real important—Claire could be in danger—who was it that called?"

She wouldn't look at me but after a while she said, "A man."

"Who?"

She shrugged. "Just a man. He asked for Mrs. Gardner."

I stared at her and she looked away. Her acned cheeks flushed.

"Then what happened?"

"She went and emptied the till and left."

"Did she seem upset?"

"Upset—how?"

"Was she scared, mad, excited—?"

Dedee gave that serious thought and finally decided that she had looked more mad than anything else. "Not everybody'd notice, but I know her better than most—"

"You sure do. Did you see which way she went when she got to the street?"

"She headed west—up the hill."

"Dedee—you're a doll," I said, and took off.

CHAPTER
21

The streetlights came on as I approached the Gardner house and I strolled easy past the front to take a look at the side street beyond. There was no Graham Paige in sight. I went and took a gander down the alley but still drew a blank. There were lights in most houses I passed, usually in the kitchen where womenfolk were cleaning up after dinner. I came to Gardner's garage which stood parallel with the alley and looked past it toward the big white house. There was no kitchen light on but I could see a faint glow from a bedroom upstairs. After making a complete circle of the house, I went up on the front porch and stood near the door, listening. All I got was an earful of cricket fiddling.

The screen door was latched. After a few seconds more of listening to crickets, I went around to the back and found the back screen latched too. In the garage I found a clothes hanger and with a few twists got it bent into shape, came back to the rear door, poked a hole through the screen and reached in with the wire. The hook lifted easily out of the eye screw and a moment later I was inside the back hall. It was blacker than an African armpit. After a few seconds I moved forward and touched the inner door with my fingertips. On my right was another door which probably led to the cellar or the pantry. I turned the knob but it was locked. I tried the door to the kitchen and was a little surprised when it opened. The kitchen was some lighter—I could look through the door on the opposite side and down a hall that led to the front entry. On my right there was an archway opening on the dining room. It took only a few seconds to move through that into the living room toward the front of the house and back to the hall and the stairway leading to the second floor. Two of the steps creaked gently under the carpeting as I crept up like a stalking cat. I kept one hand on the railing, planning to vault over if Nate appeared at the top with his sawed-off shotgun. When I was up too far for that I took about half a week between steps. My head cleared the floor level and I straightened slowly to look around. There was an open door immediately at the head of the stairs, then a hall to the right. I stepped inside the open door and looked around at a gleaming white tub, a pedestal washbasin and a toilet with its tank high on the wall. The floor was white tile.

I eased slowly along the hall toward the front bedroom door which stood open spilling light across the carpet. Two doors on my right were closed and I passed them uneasily.

Then the floor creaked loudly under my foot.

"Who's there?" called Claire.

"Wilcox," I answered. "You okay?"

There was a moment of silence and just as I was about to call again she spoke.

"Carl?"

"Yeah."

"Are you alone?"

"Yeah."

"Come here."

"Sure—are you okay?"

"I'm all right—I'm alone. I want to talk to you."

I stepped back, tried the first door and opened it. A glance inside showed nothing and I was about to try the other door when Claire called in a voice shrill with fear.

"Carl!"

I went back, paused by the door, looked through the hinge-side crack and then stuck my head around the sill.

Claire was in bed with the covers drawn up to her chin and her head raised on two pillows. A candle burned steadily on a small stand beside the bed. I looked around but saw nothing to worry me except the wardrobe in the corner on my right. It was big enough to hold a platoon and the doors were closed. All the room was neat as a parlor before a funeral.

I stepped inside, feeling skittery as a cat in a strange neighborhood.

"How'd you get in?" she asked.

"Clothes hanger through the screen," I said, looking around.

"Why didn't you knock?"

"Figured I might get my head blown off."

"It'd seem more likely to me that would happen when you made an illegal entry. What'd you expect to find?"

"Nate Larson."

She gave me a tolerant, almost kind smile.

"You keep watching the wardrobe—why don't you look inside?"

Probably I didn't believe he was there—it sure as hell would've been the dumbest thing I ever pulled to go and open those doors if I thought the bastard was waiting with his shotgun—but whatever I was thinking I made the move, poked inside among the clothes hanging there and finally returned to Claire's bedside, feeling sheepish but damned relieved.

"Bring the vanity chair over and sit down," she told me.

"You sick?" I asked as I went for the chair.

"No. I'm dying."

I looked down at the pale face, the golden hair arranged perfectly over the white pillow. She smiled wanly.

"Tell me about it," I said, and sat down.

She was lying a little to one side, facing me, with her legs bent just enough to keep her toes from sticking up. She might have rehearsed the pose before a mirror.

"You don't really believe me—do you?"

"Not often, but tell me anyway."

"I always understood you had a soft spot for widows, Carl. Have you forgotten that I'm one now?"

"No—I remember fine. Tell me what's happened—did Nate come here?"

"Yes." She turned her head a little, closed her eyes, opened them and gazed at me calmly. "He wanted money. You were right about a lot of things, Carl. You're really quite clever. I didn't realize that the first times we talked because you've squandered your abilities shamefully. You could make something of yourself if you'd just try, ever so little."

"Where's Nate, Claire?"

"Don't worry about him—he won't bother you."

"Why're you so sure?"

"He's been paid off."

"For what?"

She smiled. "Services rendered."

"Killing Flory?"

She frowned and shook her head. "Gus killed her. Really. He met her in back of the hotel where he'd wandered in his stupid, senile craving, and she told him she wasn't going to run away with him as they'd planned—she was leaving alone to join a friend in the Cities. He went crazy and hit her with his fist and when she fell, he ran away. Nate saw it all. I'd had Dedee tell Nate that Flory'd be out there, waiting for him. Before that, Dedee told Flory that Gus'd be there with something for her. She thought it'd be money to help her with the baby—"

170

"So why'd she tell Gus she was running away without him? Why didn't she just take the money?"

"Maybe you're not so clever." Claire smiled. "He didn't have any money. That's why she told him she was leaving without him."

"It sounds like you arranged for a Goddamned convention—Dedee sent Gus there too, didn't she?"

"No, I didn't plan anything like that. I just thought Nate would beat her up—I didn't think there'd be any killing—I never dreamed of that—"

"Uh-huh. So how'd Flory get her head cracked with a pipe if she was killed with Gus's fist?"

"Nate was crazy drunk and mean—when he found her on the ground he hit her with the pipe he'd brought. Can you imagine such a man? Beating a dead girl? And then you know, he left the pipe in your truck. He thought that was very clever. He thought he was clever in every way. He called Gus and told him what he'd seen and that he'd arranged things so it would look as if you were the one that did it and he wanted five hundred dollars to keep quiet."

"Did Gus pay?"

She smiled dreamily. "I let him pass on the money he was saving to run away on. He just curled up and died after that."

"I thought you said he didn't have any money?"

"He didn't, not that night. He had to arrange to get it from the bank in the Cities—"

"And then you helped Gus curl up and die, huh?"

Her eyes turned to me and her lips tightened. Then she looked up at the dim ceiling.

"What did you think of Gus?" she asked, as though we were at a tea party and she were making polite conversation.

"I thought damned little about him."

"He was a total, unmitigated weakling. In every possible way—"

"Yeah? He seems to have thrown one good punch."

"That was an accident—and he probably didn't really kill her at all—she was a sly baggage—she probably fell knowing very well he'd run away if he even suspected she was hurt. I suppose Nate lied when he said she was already dead—but what I meant about weakness was in character. Gus simply had none. He had obsessive, sneaky sexual desires, nasty, cheap—I could have made him somebody if he'd had an ounce of character. One ounce. All my life I've been burdened with characterless men—men without imagination, intelligence or strength of purpose, always susceptible to fluttery-eyed hussies, booze and cards—"

So she had hated her old man too. The hate excited her—she was fired up like a furnace in a blizzard night and her face glowed in the candlelight until suddenly she caught my expression, stopped talking and sagged back against the pillows. Then she smiled at me, all sweetness and trust.

"Would you get me a glass of water, Carl?"

"Sure."

I walked slowly to the doorway, hesitated a second and stepped into the hall. It was still empty. I passed the closed doors, carefully avoided the squeaky spot I'd hit earlier, entered the bathroom, looked behind the door and pulled on the light. A glass stood on a shelf over the pedestal sink and I filled it after letting the water run a few seconds. The water in Corden is hard enough to rattle in a sink and smells of sulfur. I wouldn't drink it on the Sahara.

I carried the glass back down the hall, still skittery as a spooked colt, and tried to plan sudden moves in case Nate appeared—which I was solid certain was going to happen.

Claire hadn't moved that I could see and she raised her

right hand as though it were weighted when I offered her the glass.

"I've been a very unlucky woman, Carl," she said. I must have looked unconvinced because she smiled, took a sip of the water and handed the glass back. I put it on the stand beside the bed as she went on.

"I know—you think anyone who lives in a decent house, eats regularly and belongs to an established family has everything she could ask—"

"Did you poison Gus?" I asked.

She studied me, looking straight into my eyes, then examined all parts of my face.

"Dying was his own idea," she said finally.

"You mean he knew what you were doing and just let it happen?"

"Gus is a very dull subject, let's talk about something else—what do you really think of me?"

"I think you're a castrating female."

She gave a short, exasperated laugh, throwing her head back, relaxed and watched me almost sleepily.

"I have never castrated a man with real—spirit."

"You never had a chance, I'd guess."

"Are you trying to say I frighten you?"

She loved the idea—which had never occurred to me—but I grinned and said maybe, a little. She rolled to her side, propped her head on her hand and smiled.

"How much of what I've told you have you really believed?"

"All that was true. Like you setting up the meeting—and even the bad-luck line. Where you goofed was having them both there. Just one would have been enough and it wouldn't have come back to you. It was a case of overdoing it. But from what I hear, you always went at things with a little extra—"

"I learned very early in politics you can never take anything for granted or plan too much—"

"You got it all wrong—you can overdo anything."

She arched her eyebrows. "Is Carl Wilcox preaching moderation now?"

"I don't mind if I do—long as I don't have to practice it."

"What do you want besides booze, girls and a fight now and then?"

"I like to travel."

"Really?" She sat up again. She was almost as busy alone in bed as Lil was with company. "Where would you like to go?"

"South Seas."

"Oh yes—blue skies, bright sun, brown-skinned girls and—what's the liquor made from coconut milk—?"

"I don't know—but I'll bet I'd like it."

"I'm sure you would. Maybe I could help you out."

"Uh-huh." I grinned at her. "I thought maybe you'd like to."

Her eagerness cooled and she frowned.

"Another blackmailer?"

"Not at all. You sounded like a lady offering a bribe and I was just being agreeable. What do I do in the way of services? Leave Corden?"

The frown faded and the smile returned. "I'm not anxious to get rid of you, Carl, but I do need a little help."

"That's okay—I like an honest proposition as well as a crooked one—what've you got in mind?"

Her eyes got a faraway look for a second. She was having a hell of a time deciding which system to use in making me trot her way because I was too weird to fit the patterns of men she'd spent her life managing.

"Remember when you came into the restaurant a couple weeks ago? You sat at the corner stool and watched me with such insolent eyes—I've never been so brazenly examined before—I wanted to slap you and at the same time I understood why you do so well with certain kinds of women—"

"I've got a hell of a lot more reputation than experience, lady, believe me."

"I suppose so. But reputations have a way of becoming reality sometimes—don't you think?"

"Could be. What the hell are we getting at?"

"Maybe we're talking a deal, Carl. You have lots of time, don't you?"

"I don't know—you said you were dying."

"I was—figuratively. I feel very alive right now. It's nice talking to you, here in my bedroom, without having to worry about anybody making a fuss or popping in. People our age are so seldom free—there are always others around—you and I have no one to concern us at all—we can do as we please tonight."

"Uh-huh. What if Orrie comes tearing back from Aquatown to see what happened to Nate when he finds out the drunk they picked up wasn't him?"

"You can hide under my bed."

"Why should I hide? I thought we were free."

"I was teasing. If he comes we'll simply tell him we haven't seen Nate and he'll go away."

And that's exactly what happened. It wasn't two minutes later when I heard Orrie's tin Lizzie out front. Claire laughed, threw back the covers and slipped out of bed. The white nightgown flowed around her slim body as smooth as water and almost as transparent and then it disappeared under a proper robe and she was sailing down the stairs like a nymph going to meet her lover. I trailed along.

Orrie clumped up the steps and stood on the porch, puffing a little and looking grim. He glared past Claire at me.

"It wasn't Nate," he said. "It was a kid looked some like

him, that's all. He didn't know where he got Nate's wallet—claimed he hadn't stolen it—probably didn't—there was hardly anything in it but a name and address card. What the hell are you doing up here?"

"I just didn't figure it was gonna be Nate in Aquatown."

"Why?"

I shrugged. "You know me, Orrie—hunch."

"He was worried about me," said Claire. She didn't like being ignored. Orrie looked at her. "He thought Nate might come up here."

"Why'd he think that?" asked Orrie.

"You know his theory—that I influenced Nate in the Flory murder."

Orrie scowled at me. "Do I know that?"

"You're the town cop—you know everything."

"Yeah? Then how come I can't find Nate?"

"You haven't thought about it enough. You checked Jenny's place yet—out at the barn?"

"No—I figured I'd best come here first—you haven't seen him, huh?"

"Not hide nor hair."

He looked at Claire who shook her head.

Orrie sighed, tipped his hat and went back to his jalopy. As he drove away, Claire laughed softly.

"Tell me the joke," I said, "I could use a laugh."

She looked at me from the corner of her eye and laughed again.

"You won't like it."

I believed her. She laughed again and walked down the hall toward the kitchen.

"I thought you figured the bedroom was cozy," I said.

"We'll go up there later. First I think we'd better get matters cleaned up."

"Like what?"

She faced me. "Where's your truck?"

176

"Behind the hotel."

"You'd better go get it."

"Yeah? You planning to move?"

"You're going to move something for me."

"Ah!"

She raised one eyebrow. "Aren't you going to ask what?"

"I don't think I have to—where is he?"

"Waiting for you. Upstairs."

"In the closed bedroom?"

"I thought you might have guessed."

"Has he got the shotgun?"

"You'll find him perfectly harmless—don't be afraid."

I stared at her and she returned my look with a challenging smile.

Going up the steps this time I remembered where they had creaked loudest and placed my feet close to the wall as I eased up to the door quiet as a slow leak. The hall, with its thick carpet, gave nothing away and I reached for the knob fairly sure I hadn't made a sound to warn him if he was waiting.

I twisted the knob, threw the door open, hit the floor on my hands and knees and rolled right. There was no shotgun blast—nothing. I came up a little slow, feeling foolish and relieved. Then I saw him, stretched on the bed as neat and straight as a coffined saint. Except for his shoes he was stark naked.

Although the room was warm, his skin was cold when I touched his cheek and I didn't need a doctor to tell me he was dead.

CHAPTER
22

I wouldn't have been surprised to find Claire drinking tea and making toast when I came downstairs but in fact she was sitting with her hands folded on the blue polka-dotted tablecloth and her laughing mood had left.

"How'd you do it?" I asked.

"What difference does it make? It was self-defense. He was drunk and meant to rape me. And Officer Buford will never believe you didn't know Nate was up there when he came to the front door and questioned you. You don't have any choice, Carl. You have to get him out of here for me."

"Uh-huh. Where'd you figure I should plant him?"

"The deserted sandpit west of town. Or the dump. The dump seems most appropriate—that's where he belongs."

I shook my head in admiration. "Everything in its proper place, huh Claire?"

Her eyes met mine, calm and steady. "You do understand—you've got to help me."

"Oh, you've got me boxed in good—but first—how about leveling with me all the way—what the hell really happened that Saturday night behind the hotel?"

"Just what you guessed—you had it all figured out."

"No, I don't think so. I can't swallow the notion that Dedee was so cute on the telephone that she managed to set up the convention you claimed. You got her to tell Flory

178

she'd get money if she waited out back of the hotel and then you set up Nate for the killing—but something got screwed up—did Nate show up too early and fall asleep waiting for her?"

"Gus did it," she said calmly. "He confessed and that's all that matters."

"Oh, Gus figured it was his fault, all right. He knew it'd never have happened except for him—but I don't believe he was ever behind the hotel that night. He just didn't have it in him to kill anybody, least of all Flory."

"He confessed." She was downright serene about that.

"Sure. How about Nate, did he confess before you killed him?"

"You're being sarcastic."

"Yeah, I wouldn't be surprised—but I don't believe Nate killed her. He'd have raped her first—that was always about the number-one thing in his mind—and girls as pretty as Flory don't come handy that often so he'd have had to get in first. That means it all boils down to sweet little Claire. You set things up and as usual the man you picked for the job fouled it up so you had to handle it yourself. I've got to hand it to you, Claire, you're a hell of a resourceful woman."

She smiled and her eyes glittered. "I didn't put the pipe in your truck, though, honestly I didn't. When I—stopped hitting her—I heard Nate moving—and I panicked. I just dropped that thing and ran. Nate picked it up and moved it and then he called and told me what he'd done and that he wanted money—".

"Okay—the blackmail part I can swallow—but not the panic. You dropped the pipe by Nate who'd passed out **waiting for Flory—you figured he'd get credit for your** work. All that really stumps me is why you decided to kill her. You had Gus hog-tied—he wouldn't have run off—

you had Flory whipped and the affair broken up—so why
kill her?"

Her eyes narrowed and her hands separated into small,
hard fists.

"If I tell you will you go get the truck?"

"Why not?"

"Promise!"

"I promise."

"All right. I'll tell you. They hadn't broken up. I was
fooled at first—or maybe I wasn't—maybe it was real for a
month—but then I noticed that Gus was getting ready for
something—I could always see through him—he was
transparent—shallow—he mooned around with that
imbecilic look that always came when he was lusting for
some cretin waitress— Then Saturday night I heard Flory
was at the dance—I knew right away that meant something and I was right—she was saying good-bye to her idiot
friends. Gus tried to avoid me all that evening until I
cornered him behind the café and told him I knew what he
was planning—that if he tried running away with her I'd
see him in jail—and her too. Oh, he was such a jellyfish!
He broke down completely—admitted they were running
away that night—he was meeting her behind the hotel at
one-thirty. He was going to leave me for that—that waitress and scullion! Can you imagine what people would've
said about that in this ant-hole town?"

Her voice got tighter with every word as she screwed
down every ounce of control to keep from screaming. For
several seconds she breathed heavily, and then she gave
me a gentle smile.

"It was a strange moment, then," she said. "You know
what it reminded me of? When I was very young and
trying to get Daddy elected governor."

She laughed. "You should have known me then, Carl.
My mind would race until it made my head hum—I loved

all the problems—working on different people in just the right way to make them do what I wanted. That Saturday night brought it all back. I thought of a dozen ways I could go—people I could use—there was Lard and Nate—I even thought of you—and then it was all very clear. Nate was drunk and lusting for Flory, Dedee was in love with Nate and would do anything I asked—and Flory was going to be out there in the dark behind the hotel, waiting for Gus at one-thirty. So I had Dedee telephone Nate—you can learn everyone's habits in Corden if you listen closely at the café so I knew he'd be at Lil's on Saturday night. I had Dedee tell Nate that Flory wanted to apologize—she was sorry that Lard had bullied him and would meet Nate behind the hotel. Nate'd never be suspicious of Dedee and he was conceited enough to believe that nonsense, especially when drunk. I told Dedee it was her chance to be alone with Nate if she got him there by twelve-thirty. She was afraid, but she did it.

"It couldn't have worked better if I'd had them all on strings. Nate came, all puffed up with liquor and pride, and when Dedee admitted Flory wouldn't be there for quite a while, he coaxed her into the west-wing basement and made love to her. Afterward—it was almost no time at all—he came up and sat down against the tree with his bottle and fell asleep. I went and put Dedee back together and told her to get home, take a bath and never breathe a word—"

"Did you tell her she'd go to prison if anybody heard what happened?"

Claire studied me a moment. "How'd you guess that?"

"She asked me about prison—it wasn't idle curiosity."

Claire smiled. "I made it rather vivid."

I shook my head. "I'll bet you did—so then what?"

"I had to wait a long time before she came. It was so dark I couldn't see my watch and I was sure she was late and then I thought she wasn't going to come at all. I even hoped she wouldn't—or anyway I tried to convince myself of that so the letdown wouldn't be too awful if she didn't—but finally she came around the corner and I was suddenly trembling. I had a length of pipe I'd found in the alley by my house—it seemed likely there'd be other pipe in back of the hotel because I'd heard your father was going to put in hot-water heat—"

"You figured on framing Nate, huh?"

"Well, didn't he deserve it?"

"I guess so—where'd you been all this time?"

"In the shadows of the corner between the garage and hotel wing—it was pitch black. I wore my black dress and a black shawl pulled over my head and across my face. When she—that waitress—stopped under the trees, I walked toward her. She heard me and turned, probably thinking it was Gus. I said, 'Sorry, my dear, but Gus couldn't come out tonight.'

"She said something stupid—like 'What do you mean?' She knew me right away. I told her Gus had decided he couldn't afford to buy a cheap waitress. She said she didn't know what I was talking about. She spoke too loudly—I was afraid she'd wake Nate or someone in the hotel so I didn't wait any longer—I took the pipe in both hands and hit her with all my strength. She fell but kept moving so I had to hit her again and again until she was still—"

Claire's eyes closed and she cupped her chin with her pale hands.

"For a long moment after, it was all still except for the crickets—they were screaming at me. I straightened up, looked around and heard Nate stirring under the tree. I wiped off the handle end of the pipe with my shawl so there'd be no prints, dropped it by the body and went home."

"What'd you tell Gus?"

She smiled again. "I told him I'd gone to meet Flory in his place—and saw Nate kill her."

"Did he believe you?"

She shrugged. "I'd guess he believed Nate did it, all right. But he probably thought I put him up to it. I didn't much care what he believed so long as he knew she was dead."

"So why'd you have to poison him?"

She opened her eyes and examined me for a couple seconds, before giving me her total-charm smile. "It seemed the kindest thing to do under the circumstances. He was quite content about it, actually—took it like a lamb—never asked a question or gave me an accusing look. I told you—he had no character at all. Not a shred. A complete and utter jellyfish."

"What'd you feed Nate?"

"A hat pin. He insisted we go upstairs and I knew what for and so I agreed and took him into the first bedroom and he started pawing me and I told him to wait—I'd put on a nightgown. He wasn't going to let me at first but finally he did and I went to the wardrobe and changed and took a hat pin from my white hat and hid it in my palm and when I came back he grabbed me so roughly I almost dropped the pin but I managed to hold on. I think he really believed I was willing—he was such a slobbering egomaniac—I kept trying to calm him and eventually persuaded him to—sort of rest his head on my bosom. Then I put the pin inside his ear and pushed very hard."

He voice was soft, almost dreamy.

"It worked beautifully. He made an awful sound and for a second I thought he'd have convulsions but suddenly he was nice and still. I pushed him off, washed the pin and put it back in my white hat, slipped on my robe and went downstairs to look around and saw you trying the front door. So I went back upstairs, closed the bedroom door on Nate, got into my own bed and waited for you."

"I'll be damned."

The confession agreed with her something wonderful—her eyes sparkled, her face was smooth and glowing. She looked pure as Jesus's mother.

"Are you going after your truck now?" she asked.

"Sure—if that'll make you believe I'm on your side."

"I know you're on my side, Carl. You always help widows—Jenny and the two before her, and now me, the fourth. You take care of Nate for me and everything will be lovely, you'll see."

"Sure. You got any hat pins in this room?"

She didn't appreciate that at all. Her face took on an injured look and she said she hoped I wasn't going to be crude. The hope sounded a little faint.

"Just one thing before I go after the truck," I said. "Where'd Nate leave the shotgun?"

"It's under the bed in the guest room. He wanted it close for when you came."

"Very thoughtful—I'd better get rid of that too."

"You can take it when you bring the truck. You can't walk down the street carrying it."

"By golly—you think of everything."

She smiled me out and I walked down the hill toward City Hall.

184

CHAPTER
23

Orrie's Ford was parked in front of City Hall and there was a light in the office but he wasn't in sight. For a few seconds I had the spooky notion that Claire had done him in too but then I remembered the cell cot and went in there and found him asleep. I came damned near locking the door on him but of course he'd have the key in his pocket so it wasn't much use. I gave him a shake.

"Wha—?" he muttered, opened his eyes and groaned.

"I got the whole story," I said.

He closed his eyes, grunted, sat up and rubbed his face with a rubbery palm.

"We got another corpse. He's in Claire's spare bedroom, naked as a jaybird and dead. I'm supposed to be getting my truck to haul him over to the dump."

"Jesus," he breathed. He stood up very carefully, arched his back, rubbed his neck and took a step before realizing he'd taken off his shoes. He sat down, slipped them on, tied the laces, stood up and trailed me into the office where he sat down heavily and stared at me. I spilled the whole story, fast.

He was plenty awake by the time I finished.

He shook his head. "I suppose it's gotta be true—it's too crazy for a lie—but I don't think there's any way to tell when that woman's giving facts and when it's dreams."

"It wasn't dreams that did in Flory, Torkelson, Gus and Nate. It was her all the way."

"Naw—Nate done it to Torky."

"Nate just made the delivery, she set it up."

He grunted agreement.

"Now you got to go arrest her. And don't forget about that shotgun under the bed."

He scowled. "I ain't forgetting that—I figure you'll take care of it. Just get your truck, go up there like she asked and park in the alley. Bring down the gun first—"

"How about the hat pin? You don't want to forget that."

"She can't stick it in my ear if she's not in reach—but that shotgun's something else. I don't like them damned things a bit. Now, you get that in the truck and see if you can talk her into giving herself up. I mean, hell, you can convince her we can't prove anything but that she done him in in self-defense—"

"Goddamnit, Orrie, nobody can convince that woman of anything she doesn't want to believe—and she's not ready to have this town know a naked man was found in her bed. This woman's always got the final argument—and I don't want any more talk with her."

He finally talked me into going after the gun. He promised he'd drive up within a block and be waiting when I came out with the piece and then he'd just walk in and arrest her. I told him that sounded damned heroic.

I drove the truck to the uphill side of Claire's block and coasted down the alley without lights. The whole neighborhood was dark and still as a bear cave in January.

The spring twanged when I pulled the screen open but inside the silence was so heavy it pressed on my eardrums. I soft-stepped through the kitchen, passed into the hall and approached the stairs.

Claire appeared in the living room entry. At first I saw only her pale face—she was dressed in black again. When she turned on a small lamp I saw the shotgun with its double muzzle pointing at the floor just short of my shoe tips.

"You took a long time," she said.

"Truck needed gas," I lied. "Had to siphon some from my old man's car—couldn't find a hose."

"Why didn't you just take his car?"

"He's got the keys."

She nodded absentmindedly. She knew I was lying and didn't want to learn what it meant. "Let's get on with it."

It didn't seem like the time to ask that she give herself up so I climbed the stairs and she followed about a yard behind. I had a pretty clear notion of what she planned— she'd leave me healthy until Nate was on the truck, and it didn't seem likely she'd blast me in town, so I was fairly safe if I stayed careful and Orrie was prompt.

It was some relief to find the body still limp and I used a fireman's carry but before I left the room Claire pointed to a sack and told me to bring that too—it was Nate's clothing. By then she'd raised the muzzle of the shotgun high enough for me to lose all interest in debate. I struggled down the stairs and out the back door, cowed as a Marine recruit, but still expecting rescue from good old Orrie.

He didn't show outside the back door and I figured, okay, he's waiting by the truck.

Only he wasn't.

I had the sand rig on my truck then because my last job had been hauling gravel for the county and that meant it was a hell of a chore getting Nate's carcass up into the box.

"Okay," I said after the grunt work, "gimme the shotgun and I'll toss it in front and take off."

She shook her head. The twin barrels were pointed at my gut and the openings looked big enough to roll watermelons down.

"I'm coming along," she said.

"No need—"

"I'm coming. Is there a shovel in the truck?"

I admitted there was and started cussing Orrie in my mind. Then I figured, what the hell, argue.

"Look, Claire, you're gonna get caught—why not just fess up to Orrie—tell 'im Nate was trying to rape you—"

The shotgun muzzles looked even bigger when she pointed them at my head.

"Get in the truck, Carl."

"Yes ma'am."

I started around the hood but she halted me and said I should climb straight in and crawl across to the driver's seat. When I did, she followed, keeping the shotgun pointed at my middle. Once inside she rested the gun butt against the door and watched me with steady eyes.

"Let's go," she ordered.

I started the engine and in the quiet night it seemed loud enough to wake the dead but no lights came on in the neighboring houses. As we pulled out of the alley and turned left my hopes jumped at the sight of Orrie's Ford driving up the hill on my right.

"Hurry!" said Claire, who'd seen the lights.

"If you wanna hurry, you'd be better off outside the truck," I told her.

"Don't try to be funny—start shifting."

It was a great race—like two crippled turtles climbing a sandy slope.

I turned left at the first corner and headed for open country while Orrie came chugging after. The outside mirrors gave Claire and me equal views of the pursuit but there was no way for Claire to shoot because the sand rig on the back blocked the rear window and jutted out too far for a shot from the side. I was sorry about the last—nothing could've simplified life more than her leaning out the window with the shotgun.

She kept it pointed at me and watched the mirror with quick glances. I couldn't see any sign of panic. Not in her.

I kept watching the gun, trying to figure my chances of knocking it aside, and while it was sure close enough to reach, the slightest nudge would make her shoot and things were too damned cozy in that cab for me to think that ricochets wouldn't raise hell even if she missed me clean.

Claire looked at my feet and wanted to know why the truck wouldn't go faster. I said it was going uphill. She doubted that was the reason but wasn't foolish enough to blast me yet.

Orrie swung into the left lane and started pulling up on me.

"Run him off the road," said Claire.

"Aw—"

"Turn!"

He wasn't far enough alongside to make it murder so I eased over and crowded him until he hit his brakes and dropped back. A couple seconds later I heard a popping sound and the truck shuddered.

"That's it, lady," I said, "he's just shot out my tires."

"All right," she said, calm as if she were talking to a cabdriver in front of church, "just pull over here and stop."

"Jesus, I sure wish you'd had that notion before he blew my tires to hell."

"Get out as soon as you set the brake," she told me. She was great on details.

"Then what?" We had almost lumped to a stop but I knew damned well she wasn't through yet.

"Then you get out on that side and I'll follow."

I figured she had several notions about what she was going to do but it seemed most likely she'd shoot Orrie, take his gun, finish me and then report it all as a shoot-out.

I opened my door, made sure she was following close,

stepped to the gravel and let my leg go limp. The next second I was under the truck and rolling.

"She's got the shotgun!" I yelled at Orrie.

I scrambled to knees and elbows and scooted for the rear, got clear and made a dive for the ditch which wasn't deep enough to hide a gopher. I hit the weeds on hands and knees and kept going for several seconds before the loud silence behind me caught up and left me feeling foolish.

After some hard breathing I peeked back at the truck, which squatted on flat rear tires at the edge of the road with its headlight beams already filled by swirling bugs and their shadows. A dog on the nearest farm was barking excitedly and another dog, farther away, took it up. There was no moon but every star in creation was working at full power.

In a minute or so my heart slowed down and I could hear voices from the far side of the truck. It was hard to figure what kind of chatter could go on between two people pointing guns at each other but they sure as hell weren't shooting and nobody seemed to care where I was. Orrie sounded outraged, Claire's voice was only a murmur.

I worked slowly back until I was close enough to hear.

"I can't do that, Claire, Goddamnit—pardon me—but Goddamnit it wouldn't be right—"

"It won't mean a thing to him and it'll save everybody a lot of trouble—what possible difference can it make?"

"It'd get out—a thing like that—somehow—"

"Don't be ridiculous. Call Wilcox back—see if he doesn't agree with me. There's simply no alternative. I can't miss you from here—and you can't make yourself shoot first— so stop being childish and let's have an agreement—"

Orrie sputtered some more without saying anything, finally gave up and hollered for me.

I was standing about a yard behind the rear truck wheel. Claire was no more than five feet beyond Orrie.

"Quit hollering," I said, "I'm right here."

Orrie was rattled to hear me that close—he probably hoped I was halfway to town after help—but he didn't turn and he kept his gun pointing at Claire.

"How much've you heard?" he asked.

"She's got a proposition you don't like—what is it?"

"She'll turn herself in if I'll put a bullet hole in Nate and say I caught him trying to sneak into her house."

"She'll admit she killed Flory?"

"Uh-huh."

"And Torkelson?"

"No. She says that was Nate."

"How about Gus."

"No. Just Flory."

"She's gonna admit she picked up a hunk of pipe and smashed that kid to hell but she's squeamish about people knowing her hat-pin trick, huh?"

"Well, she'll admit she put Nate up to killing Flory—that's all."

"What the hell good is shooting a dead man gonna do you and me?"

"It might keep you both from getting killed," said Claire.

"*Might?*"

"I didn't mean it that way—it *will* keep you from getting killed."

"You're not gonna kill this kid," I told her.

"I'll get Buford."

I didn't doubt her for a second. While thinking it over I squatted to see if she could spot my legs under the corner of the sand rack. It was too dark to make her out so I figured I was in fair shape.

"Let me get this straight," I said. "You want us to unload Nate, drill him in a likely spot, and then hand out a story claiming he was shot to keep him from depurifying you?"

"You'll have to take him back to town and shoot him there. So people will hear the shot."

"That ought to lock it up good. Everybody'll know he planned murder or rape because he's only wearing shoes."

"You'll dress him—before you shoot him."

"My God," said Orrie indignantly, "she's thought of everything."

Not quite. She'd forgotten the tires had been shot off the truck and Orrie was driving a Model T coupe that'd hardly hold two people, let alone three live ones plus a corpse and a shotgun. Or more likely, she didn't care about those details because the second Orrie turned the gun away she'd blast him.

"Run it through for me again," I said. "I just don't get the picture."

She was willing. While she talked I slipped off my shoes, climbed the sand rig back, lowered myself inside and hustled to the front, almost stumbling over Nate in my rush. When I peeked over the edge I saw a flash of light from the west. I inched up further and saw Claire a little to my right with the shotgun held tight up to her shoulder. She hadn't seen the light behind her.

"Here comes a car," said Orrie.

She jerked her head around and the motion pulled the shotgun away from Orrie. I went over the side and dropped on her.

My left foot hit the barrel and my right knee caught her shoulder. The gun went off, blasting sand and gravel, and Claire screamed so loud the combination racket about numbed me but I didn't have time for rest. She was like an eight-legged wildcat having a fit and it seemed half an hour before Orrie got the cuffs on her. Then we just hung on until the car we'd seen came up and Orrie flagged the driver down.

CHAPTER
24

Claire wasn't in a chatty mood when we got her back to City Hall and Orrie didn't waste a lot of time trying to charm her out of it. When she was safely locked up we walked out front for a smoke.

"What the hell took you so long getting up to the Gardner house?" I asked.

"When I came outside I had a flat. Front left. Nothing to do but change it."

"You damned near got me killed—about ten seconds later and it'd been my ass."

"That's right. But I'd have had her cold, then. She couldn't talk her way out of killing you."

"That'd make it a lot simpler, huh? Sorry I loused you up."

"I'd have given you full credit for solving the case, Carl."

I knew just how he'd do it, too—like a bighearted slob, lying to be noble so everybody'd know he was lying and would say what a great guy he was, giving credit to that Wilcox bum.

"Well," he said, "you gonna tell Jenny about Nate?"

"Hell no. The way things are between us, it wouldn't be any easier for her and it'd be a hell of a lot harder for me. Do your own job, once."

He gave his martyr's sigh and squinted against the smoke rising from his cigar.

"Knocking a woman around puts you in a bad mood," he told me. "All right, I'll see Jenny tomorrow—no use spoiling her sleep—right?"

I nodded, dropped my cigarette butt and stepped on it. "Did you really have somebody that claimed they saw me out back of the hotel that Saturday night?"

"Naw—it just seemed worth a try."

"You didn't ever really figure I'd done it, did you?"

"Well, it did seem a little likely right off. I mean—the minute you come back and I knew Flory was there in the hotel—I was wondering how long before you knocked her up. And then, finding her out there like that—it made me so Goddamned mad I wanted it settled quick—you know? If it'd been you, everything would've been nice and simple and I wasn't in any mood for a lot of horsing around—"

"So I was your patsy."

"Well, you sure were handy, but I'll tell you one thing, Carl, if I'd really figured you'd done it, I'd have had my gun out when I come up to your room. You ain't a man I take a chance with."

He meant it for a compliment—it was easier than apologizing.

"You sleepy?" I asked.

"Naw."

"Let's go see Boswell."

He took about half a second to think that over and then grunted and we started walking.

"Now what're you gonna do?" he asked. "For a living, I mean."

"What do you figure I'd ought to do?"

"Go somewhere and start fresh."

"I'm too ripe to start fresh."

"No you ain't—you could do lots of things."

I didn't bother to ask him what.

"You'd ought to think of your future," he insisted.

194

"I got it all planned. I'm gonna hang one on tonight, and tomorrow, when I feel up to it, I'll mosey over to the city and look up that widow that runs the hardware store."

He shook his head. "You're a born bum, Carl, that's all."

"Well, it beats being unemployed."

MORE MYSTERIOUS PLEASURES

HAROLD ADAMS

MURDER

Carl Wilcox debuts in a story of triple murder which exposes the underbelly of corruption in the town of Corden, shattering the respectability of its most dignified citizens. #501 $3.50

THE NAKED LIAR

When a sexy young widow is framed for the murder of her husband, Carl Wilcox comes through to help her fight off cops and big-city goons. #420 $3.95

THE FOURTH WIDOW

Ex-con/private eye Carl Wilcox is back, investigating the death of a "popular" widow in the Depression-era town of Corden, S.D. #502 $3.50

EARL DERR BIGGERS

THE HOUSE WITHOUT A KEY

Charlie Chan debuts in the Honolulu investigation of an expatriate Bostonian's murder. #421 $3.95

THE CHINESE PARROT

Charlie Chan works to find the key to murders seemingly without victims—but which have left a multitude of clues. #503 $3.95

BEHIND THAT CURTAIN

Two murders sixteen years apart, one in London, one in San Francisco, each share a major clue in a pair of velvet Chinese slippers. Chan seeks the connection. #504 $3.95

THE BLACK CAMEL

When movie goddess Sheila Fane is murdered in her Hawaiian pavilion, Chan discovers an interrelated crime in a murky Hollywood mystery from the past. #505 $3.95

CHARLIE CHAN CARRIES ON

An elusive transcontinental killer dogs the heels of the Lofton Round the World Cruise. When the touring party reaches Honolulu, the murderer finally meets his match. #506 $3.95

JAMES M. CAIN
THE ENCHANTED ISLE
A beautiful runaway is involved in a deadly bank robbery in this posthumously published novel. #415 $3.95

CLOUD NINE
Two brothers—one good, one evil—battle over a million-dollar land deal and a luscious 16-year-old in this posthumously published novel. #507 $3.95

ROBERT CAMPBELL
IN LA-LA LAND WE TRUST
Child porn, snuff films, and drunken TV stars in fast cars—that's what makes the L.A. world go 'round. Whistler, a luckless P.I., finds that it's not good to know too much about the porn trade in the City of Angels. #508 $3.95

GEORGE C. CHESBRO
VEIL
Clairvoyant artist Veil Kendry volunteers to be tested at the Institute for Human Studies and finds that his life is in deadly peril; is he threatened by the Institute, the Army, or the CIA? #509 $3.95

WILLIAM L. DeANDREA
THE LUNATIC FRINGE
Police Commissioner Teddy Roosevelt and Officer Dennis Muldoon comb 1896 New York for a missing exotic dancer who holds the key to the murder of a prominent political cartoonist. #306 $3.95.

SNARK
Espionage agent Bellman must locate the missing director of British Intelligence—and elude a master terrorist who has sworn to kill him. #510 $3.50

KILLED IN THE ACT
Brash, witty Matt Cobb, TV network troubleshooter, must contend with bizarre crimes connected with a TV spectacular—one of which is a murder committed before 40 million witnesses. #511 $3.50

KILLED WITH A PASSION
In seeking to clear an old college friend of murder, Matt Cobb must deal with the Mad Karate Killer and the Organic Hit Man, among other eccentric criminals. #512 $3.50

KILLED ON THE ICE
When a famous psychiatrist is stabbed in a Manhattan skating rink, Matt Cobb finds it necessary to protect a beautiful Olympic skater who appears to be the next victim. #513 $3.50

JAMES ELLROY
SUICIDE HILL
Brilliant L.A. Police sergeant Lloyd Hopkins teams up with the FBI to solve a series of inside bank robberies—but is he working with or against them? #514 $3.95

PAUL ENGLEMAN
CATCH A FALLEN ANGEL
Private eye Mark Renzler becomes involved in publishing mayhem and murder when two slick mens' magazines battle for control of the lucrative market. #515 $3.50

LOREN D. ESTLEMAN
ROSES ARE DEAD
Someone's put a contract out on freelance hit man Peter Macklin. Is he as good as the killers on his trail? #516 $3.95

ANY MAN'S DEATH
Hit man Peter Macklin is engaged to keep a famous television evangelist *alive*—quite a switch from his normal line. #517 $3.95

DICK FRANCIS
THE SPORT OF QUEENS
The autobiography of the celebrated race jockey/crime novelist.
#410 $3.95

JOHN GARDNER
THE GARDEN OF WEAPONS
Big Herbie Kruger returns to East Berlin to uncover a double agent. He confronts his own past and life's only certainty—death.
#103 $4.50

BRIAN GARFIELD
DEATH WISH
Paul Benjamin is a modern-day New York vigilante, stalking the rapist-killers who victimized his wife and daughter. The basis for the Charles Bronson movie. #301 $3.95

DEATH SENTENCE
A riveting sequel to *Death Wish*. The action moves to Chicago as Paul Benjamin continues his heroic (or is it psychotic?) mission to make city streets safe. #302 $3.95

TRIPWIRE
A crime novel set in the American West of the late 1800s. Boag, a black outlaw, seeks revenge on the white cohorts who left him for dead. "One of the most compelling characters in recent fiction."—Robert Ludlum. #303 $3.95

FEAR IN A HANDFUL OF DUST
Four psychiatrists, three men and a woman, struggle across the blazing Arizona desert—pursued by a fanatic killer they themselves have judged insane. "Unique and disturbing."—Alfred Coppel. #304 $3.95

JOE GORES
A TIME OF PREDATORS
When Paula Halstead kills herself after witnessing a horrid crime, her husband vows to avenge her death. Winner of the Edgar Allan Poe Award. #215 $3.95

COME MORNING
Two million in diamonds are at stake, and the ex-con who knows their whereabouts may have trouble staying alive if he turns them up at the wrong moment. #518 $3.95

NAT HENTOFF
BLUES FOR CHARLIE DARWIN
Gritty, colorful Greenwich Village sets the scene for Noah Green and Sam McKibbon, two street-wise New York cops who are as at home in jazz clubs as they are at a homicide scene.
#208 $3.95

THE MAN FROM INTERNAL AFFAIRS
Detective Noah Green wants to know who's stuffing corpses into East Village garbage cans . . . and who's lying about him to the Internal Affairs Division. #409 $3.95

PATRICIA HIGHSMITH
THE BLUNDERER
An unhappy husband attempts to kill his wife by applying the murderous methods of another man. When things go wrong, he pays a visit to the more successful killer—a dreadful error. #305 $3.95

DOUG HORNIG
THE DARK SIDE
Insurance detective Loren Swift is called to a rural commune to investigate a carbon-monoxide murder. Are the commune inhabitants as gentle as they seem? #519 $3.95

P.D. JAMES/T.A. CRITCHLEY
THE MAUL AND THE PEAR TREE
The noted mystery novelist teams up with a police historian to create a fascinating factual account of the 1811 Ratcliffe Highway murders.
#520 $3.95

STUART KAMINSKY'S "TOBY PETERS" SERIES
NEVER CROSS A VAMPIRE
When Bela Lugosi receives a dead bat in the mail, Toby tries to catch the prankster. But Toby's time is at a premium because he's also trying to clear William Faulkner of a murder charge! #107 $3.95

HIGH MIDNIGHT

When Gary Cooper and Ernest Hemingway come to Toby for protection, he tries to save them from vicious blackmailers. #106 $3.95

HE DONE HER WRONG

Someone has stolen Mae West's autobiography, and when she asks Toby to come up and see her sometime, he doesn't know how deadly a visit it could be. #105 $3.95

BULLET FOR A STAR

Warner Brothers hires Toby Peters to clear the name of Errol Flynn, a blackmail victim with a penchant for young girls. The first novel in the acclaimed Hollywood-based private eye series. #308 $3.95

THE FALA FACTOR

Toby comes to the rescue of lady-in-distress Eleanor Roosevelt, and must match wits with a right-wing fanatic who is scheming to overthrow the U.S. Government. #309 $3.95

JOSEPH KOENIG
FLOATER

Florida Everglades sheriff Buck White matches wits with a Miami murder-and-larceny team who just may have hidden his ex-wife's corpse in a remote bayou. #521 $3.50

ELMORE LEONARD
THE HUNTED

Long out of print, this 1974 novel by the author of *Glitz* details the attempts of a man to escape killers from his past. #401 $3.95

MR. MAJESTYK

Sometimes bad guys can push a good man too far, and when that good guy is a Special Forces veteran, everyone had better duck. #402 $3.95

THE BIG BOUNCE

Suspense and black comedy are cleverly combined in this tale of a dangerous drifter's affair with a beautiful woman out for kicks. #403 $3.95

ELSA LEWIN
I, ANNA

A recently divorced woman commits murder to avenge her degradation at the hands of a sleazy lothario. #522 $3.50

THOMAS MAXWELL
KISS ME ONCE

An epic *roman noir* which explores the romantic but seamy underworld of New York during the WWII years. When the good guys are off fighting in Europe, the bad guys run amok in America. #523 $3.95

DAVID WILLIAMS' "MARK TREASURE" SERIES
UNHOLY WRIT
London financier Mark Treasure helps a friend reaquire some property. He stays to unravel the mystery when a Shakespeare manuscript is discovered and foul murder done. #112 $3.95

TREASURE BY DEGREES
Mark Treasure discovers there's nothing funny about a board game called "Funny Farms." When he becomes involved in the takeover struggle for a small university, he also finds there's nothing funny about murder. #113 $3.95

■ ■